THE BUCKET LIST

EMELLE ADAMS

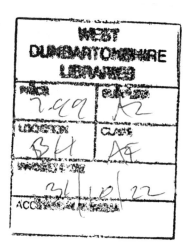

Thanks to:
Adam, John, Mum and Dave, and Maria

With contributions from:
Louise, Jenifer, Georgie, and Karen

ONE

I am furious, and I want everyone else to be too! My illness is 100 per cent terminal, but last time I checked, we all have a terminal illness—it's called life.

I want to tell my story, which is why I started this journal. Most people live their life as if it's endless. I'm sorry to break it to you like this, but (surprise, surprise) it's not.

I should focus on being positive. I should talk about smiling in the face of death. I should spend my time laughing, making memories. I'd get a lot more sympathy if I did, if I accepted my impending doom with dignified grace.

I've always wished I could be more graceful. Grace makes others feel more comfortable. People want that. They want optimism. They want to believe none of us are facing our expiry date.

I am going to die soon—perhaps next year, or the next, or the next again. I might be blind, incontinent, and immobile prior to that. What will they say when I finally snuff it? Maybe they'll say, 'Thoughts and prayers. She's in a better place now. Amen.'

We all want to be remembered well. In fact, being remembered at all would be great. But I'm so glad I won't have to see all the platitudes on social media. The emojis!

How has someone's existence boiled down to a love heart or a crying yellow face? Is that it? Just pressing a modified 'Like' button on your phone? Not even a 'With Sympathy' card? However, I don't want 'Thinking about you', 'Love to you and all the family', or 'Sorry for your loss', and I won't be in a better place.

I'm a terrible person—so selfish, so irritable that I even annoy myself. I'm pitiful. I have no self-control. Also, why am I so bloody angry all the time?

TWO

BEFORE I GOT ILL, John and I went out with Susan and Paul for dinner. Susan had come down from the island for work, and Paul had some time off, so they made a weekend of it.

I chose a bar in Edinburgh, on George Street. I dressed up, or so I thought, until I saw all the glamorous young people taking selfies for Instagram. I had worn my Moschino boots matched with my Vivienne Westwood handbag. Some women can wear a bin bag and look a million dollars. I wear designer and look like I stole it from a jumble sale.

I stared at the table of impossibly slim girls next to us for a prolonged time, wondering what they might order. Feeling round in comparison, I ordered steamed fish and vegetables, a healthy, less-calorific choice. That kind of meal would be boring at home, but I hoped the restaurant would spice it up. The slender girls opposite were all served enormous burgers and chips. I was astonished, although I considered that they might not have eaten all day. Their phones came out—when I say 'came out', their phones had never made it into their bags or pockets—as they styled and snapped photographs of themselves and their food. They chatted, comparing the photos, retaking them to suit. Then they left.

'They didn't eat their burgers,' I whispered to Susan, who didn't look like she had noticed them. Without giving them a glance or looking up from her menu, she commented, 'They've never eaten a burger in their lives.' Pausing, she flipped the menu over—a special half-priced one that meant the evening meal cost a mere ten pounds. 'One of them nibbled a piece of lettuce.'

Each area of the bar was adorned with stunning backdrops, with an outside bar area lit for exterior shots. The girls teetered off on heels, phone cameras in hand. They were living the high life, enjoying life to the fullest. Or were they? Eating and drinking and having fun just for show. A facade for followers and friends to see.

Our meals arrived, and Susan began to tell a story about a celebrity she had seen in town.

'I can't stand him,' John butted in.

'Oh, I like him. Why?' asked Susan, toying with her pasta.

'I just can't.'

'Oh, he's got a list.' I interjected.

'A list?' Susan narrowed her eyes.

'Yeah, a list of celebrities he doesn't like. As soon as any of them come on the TV, he says, "He's on the list," or "She's on the list." There are loads of them. We can hardly watch anything,' I explained.

'Paul has a list. Don't you?' She glanced sideways at him and took a bite of penne. He didn't answer, just gave her a look back.

'I've Got a Little List ...' I started the song from *The Mikado*, which clearly neither of them recognised, so I stopped.

'If the world were going to end, I've a list of people to, you know, *deal with*,' Paul muttered. It was clear his was not a list of people from the telly who got on his nerves—this was a list of enemies getting a dose of revenge.

Susan rolled her eyes as he spoke and then raised her eyebrows at me. Holding grudges and taking revenge was not up her street. In fact, she might have hoped I'd tell him off for such a terrible idea. Instead, I decided to take Paul's path in this line of conversation.

'What would you do?' I asked.

'I'm not sure exactly, Angela,' he confessed to me. 'Just make sure they'd hurt in those last moments on Earth.'

'Would you kill them?'

Susan shook her head and took another sip of wine.

Paul shrugged and winked. 'Well, it's the end of the world, so it wouldn't matter.'

'Suppose you were dying ...' I said. They both stared at me. 'If you only had so many months to live, would you kill them in that scenario? Would you do them in then?'

'Well, no.' Paul shook his head. 'I'm *potentially* killing them.'

Susan groaned.

'Sorry, Susan, but they're going to die anyway because a meteor is headed for Earth ...' He waved a hand. 'Or whatever else is ending the world.'

'Oh, I was thinking more along the lines that you didn't want them outliving you, and you wouldn't get jailed for it. More of a nothing-to-lose scenario.' I laughed. Paul and Susan didn't.

'I'll be sleeping with one eye open tonight!' joked John, changing the subject as the waiter came to ask how our meals were.

While we were eating, the girls from the next table must have been taking more photos elsewhere in the establishment. They were still posing outside when we left. It was a Tuesday night, and they were red-carpet ready. If I had seen one wearing a tiara, I would not have been surprised. I suddenly wished I were cancer Instagram ready.

THREE

> I am Miss Brain Tumour 2018, and I want a crown, dammit, and a sash to go with it!
>
> 'She's so brave and inspiring,' they will say.
>
> 'She's fighting it.'
>
> 'The biggest battle ...'
>
> How many war metaphors are associated with cancer? You must fight it, although there is bugger all you can do about it.
>
> Your battle is waking up and going to the hospital. Your courage is continuing to exist. In the end, you win or lose. 'Well done, you!' Or a tsked, 'Such a pity.'
>
> Some take a defeatist attitude towards this disease. Once you face it, that's it. You must accept it, endure it with a smile. Then there is my attitude—flaming anger.
>
> Over the years, my boiling temper calmed to a mild simmer. Recently, however, this diagnosis has notched it up to such a level I could detonate. It's the stress of the end being near, I imagine.
>
> Sometimes, the urge to hit someone in the face with

a metal object is almost overwhelming. Often, I chant the words to 'The Trolley Song' by Judy Garland while I furiously clean to turn the heat down on my rage. I change the words so the trolley doesn't clang; the frying pan does.

I call my tumour 'Brian'. Brian and brain, get it? I like anagrams, crossword puzzles, quizzes, and games. I'm a geek. Geeks are sexy these days, except for female ones.

I think of the snail named Brian from The Magic Roundabout. *It's a pleasant memory. I used to watch the show on a massive TV that heated up our living room. No remote back then—you had to press the buttons down hard to change the channel.*

Brian on the television was cute, but this one is living in my damn head. I suppose all the memories I have in there will go anyway. Won't be able to say, 'Well, here's my fun fact of the day' anymore.

Brian approves of trivia and of all the life-affirming memes and quotes I read. He is a benign, positive factor in my life, apart from slowly killing me over time.

Brian was diagnosed six years ago. Like most brain tumours, he's incurable. The point of treatment is to keep me alive, offer me the best possible quality of life. Brain tumours aren't that different from other types of cancer. Over time, the cancer cells invade the normal brain tissue around them. No surgery can remove them all, so they always grow back as a new tumour. Brian already has.

He was initially a grade-two tumour that was successfully operated on. After observation, he, rather predictably, grew back from his residual specks to the point where doctors advised surgery again ... then radiation ... then chemotherapy for a while.

Now I'm grade three. I'm progressing. There is no certificate to hang on your wall for that, not like the one I received for piano exams.

I finished chemotherapy three months ago. The doctors wouldn't map out my future for me, but they told me reappearances happen at shorter intervals every time. It took four years the first time. Brian will return in less than four now, and two have already passed.

One day, Brian will reappear as a grade four, at which point doctors will start talking about experimental treatments, and I will book a trip to Lourdes. From what I have calculated, I'm looking at single figures when it comes to years of survival.

FOUR

A FEW YEARS BACK, before Brian emerged, Jill and Jen from work were in the tearoom. A client had not turned up, so we had a whole twenty minutes to chat on my birthday.

'Well, you are on the countdown to fifty.' (Actually, I was barely in my forties.) 'What are your plans?' asked Jen.

'For my fiftieth, I'd like to stay in a castle and pretend I'm a princess,' I answered. They laughed at that. 'I need a grand staircase to swan down, like a Hollywood star in a period drama, or I suppose someone more British, as I'll pick a castle locally. I'm not going far when Scotland is teeming with castles.'

'Is that it?' asked Jill.

'And before I turn fifty, I want to go to Africa. Botswana, Zambia, and Zimbabwe, I think. And to see Victoria Falls. I've seen safaris online. I like elephants. Do you know they tracked elephants, and when Botswana had a hunting ban, all the elephants knew not to cross the border?' They were not interested in my fun fact of the day.

'Okay, that's all very well. Let's make a list.' Jen grabbed a piece of paper and a pen. 'How about 50 Things to Do Before You're 50?' She scrawled the title at the top.

I wrote down the castle, the safari, and the elephants, and then I was stumped.

'How about your funeral plans?' Jen giggled. 'They'll need to be in place.'

'Charming! Budapest—I've never been there.'

'And there's a cheap flight from Edinburgh. Nice,' interjected Jill.

'Iceland! I'd like to go there.'

'Iceland? The supermarket? What for? To buy a prawn ring and a wee paella mix?' suggested Jen, laughing.

'Yeah, get some sausage rolls while you're at it. We'll come round,' Jill chimed in.

I laughed. 'Not the supermarket, the country!'

'Walking with alpacas' got scrawled on the list because Jen said she'd like to after she saw it in a magazine. I wrote it down. It sounded all right, and I had never done it before, although I guessed camel rides in Lanzarote and Tunisia were similar. I dithered over that, but I left the alpacas on there anyway.

'The problem is you have done so much. It'd help if you were more boring. Everything we come up with, you've already done: sung in a band, been on a cruise, been to New York.' Jen checked them off on her fingers.

'How about be an extra in a film?' I suggested. 'I put my name down for that in an agency years ago but never had the time.'

'Write your memoirs,' shouted Jill from back in her office across the corridor.

'You've always got stories to tell. I'm not sure if you are making them all up, mind you,' added Jen.

'I add embellishments here and there.' I sniffed.

We ran out of items for the list at about twenty and got back to work.

FIVE

In some strange way, knowing that Brian was incurable from the start helped me. I'm a doer, inquisitive and very logical. A 'What's the problem?' and 'How do we fix it?' person. It's the geek in me. A puzzle is just a problem that needs solving, after all.

A boyfriend once told me he couldn't show me love by helping me or doing anything for me, which left him feeling pointless. He said it was because, and I quote, 'You are too capable.' It seemed like the most complimentary criticism ever.

When I was diagnosed, I wanted to know the truth from the start. I wanted as much information as possible, to take the stress out of the situation. I wanted to know the average survival rate so I knew where I stood. I would hate wondering, not knowing. Uncertainty adds to my worry.

Except for the side-effects of the radiation and chemotherapy and a slight weakness in my left leg and arm, I've been symptom-free.

Brian lives on the right side of my brain, which controls the movement of the left limbs. On a bad day, that means feebleness and a limp on that side. On a good day, on most days, I don't even notice it.

I can manage things, but what should I do? Should I tick off the items on my bucket list?

It's pathetic. I have so little time, and I can't decide how to use it, which is hell for a doer.

I'm like that on holiday, ending up bored. When I'm at work, I gaze out of the window, daydreaming of all the things I'll see and experience. I watch others having fun and want to be in their place. But when I get the chance to, it's a disappointment. I get more of a thrill wishing for experiences than doing them.

I took a lot of time off work sick, and I thought I could get on with all those things I didn't have time to do. I enjoyed writing the lists—DIY, cleaning, sorting.

I need to clean again. That tile is cracked, and that skirting could use a lick of paint again. Being inside all the time, especially when I was poorly, I thought I'd get a thrill from the flat being fixed up. It ended in disappointment. It doesn't look any better to me now. Either that or I'm focusing on all the imperfections— that's all I can stare at all day.

I used to think of what I would achieve if only I had the time. Then, off work and with all the bloody time in the world, I couldn't come up with anything! I could achieve nothing!

Death is a dirty double-crosser, isn't it? I am livid about it. But I've been anxious all my life, angry too, with the too-many people and events that have made it worse. The damage others caused me along the way.

'She's got a bad temper,' I would overhear people say. But they would, too, if they were me. My anger

comes from being scared, being rooted in fear. Is it a cliché to say I am a cornered rat?

People wonder what goes through someone's mind when they're terminally ill. The answer is the usual rubbish interspersed with random thoughts about not living. What will being dead be like? What will I miss in the world? Then, in a blink, I forgot to buy garlic for the risotto. Or Where did I put my phone?

What will I miss? When I'm dead, I don't think I'll lie there missing things. I mean: What will happen next that I won't see? What's tomorrow's news? What's the next chapter of the world? I've seen all the latest episodes. I've seen enough history. But I'll miss the sequel. The new bits.

It's like not finishing a series on TV or when the last page of the book is torn out or the power goes out before the end of a film. What was the point even starting it?

SIX

I'M NOT keen on the book I started yesterday. Should I give up or continue reading? I decide to get that bucket list back out and add to it.

I got some money for Christmas, so I'll use it to buy a lovely notepad and pen. I love stationery. It helps to write about Brian. I don't need any excuse to buy stationery at WHSmith's. I used to love the smell of that part of Woolies when I was a Saturday girl. I was always tidying it.

I decide I'll do Jen and Jill's '50 Things to Do Before 50' list. I don't actually want to walk with alpacas, but I enjoy checking things off lists. Then I wonder, *What if I'm dead before then? What if I'm in a wheelchair for my fiftieth birthday party? Will I even have a party?* I know someone who had a 'Before I Die' party.

Should I write about my life instead? Pen the memoirs Jill and Jen said to write? That way, I could be the heroine of a book.

I laugh. A fat, average-looking, brown-haired, middle-aged woman isn't your usual heroine. But I need to get on with it. I don't want to wait until my bones are full of tumours to start doing it. I wonder if that's going to hurt. I wonder if it'll hurt simply to exist, like it did for Nadine. It's been almost two years since she died.

I check out Facebook again to see, but I end up on a *Daily Mail* site about the Royal Family. I don't care for them, but it's mind-numbing enough to serve a purpose. What age is the Queen again? I can't believe she's going to outlive me—the bloody Queen, outliving me!

SEVEN

 Miss Moleman will outlive me. Mark will outlive me. Patrick will outlive me. Eric will outlive me. Kate, Tom, Linda and Debbie, all of them will outlive me. All of them get to see what happens next. How is that fair?

I wanted to dance on their graves, not the other way around. Though, they won't care. I bet they won't even know or notice I'm gone. I bet they find out in a chance conversation, years later in the supermarket, maybe in Iceland.

'Did you know Angela died?'

'Oh, did she?'

I'll be reduced to small talk. Those narcissists, sociopaths, and downright psychopaths will reduce my existence to something as insignificant as the weather.

They can get on with planning their own funerals years in advance without a thought for me. When they die, they will get the same social media platitudes as me. How rude is that? How dare they! 'Thoughts and prayers' for those bastards—are you kidding me?

I'll finish the bucket list, all right. Instead of walking with alpacas and going to Budapest, I'll make it my hit list. I'll make it my list of those who don't deserve to see the next chapter. I'll list all those who don't deserve to live beyond my time, all those who won't see the Queen's funeral. A list of enemies, like Paul's.

They should all be grateful that I remember them at all, when they've all forgotten me.

EIGHT

I FIND the original '50 By 50' list to look at, and then I grab some paper out of the drawer to jot down ideas on, just until I get a proper fancy notebook. The paper is Trump notepaper I stole from the hotel I stayed at in New York. I say 'steal', but you are meant to take those things, aren't you? They're gifts, the pens and notepaper and all the toiletries. I'd hide them in my bag every day, so housekeeping would top them up. I took all I could, but I stopped at the dressing gowns— that's plain rude. I took the slippers, though. After all, my feet had been in them; they wouldn't use them again. It'd be unhygienic.

The names I have jotted down aren't in any order; they are just as they popped into my head. I'll work through the list again later, more logically, starting at the beginning.

'Hiya? Angela! Angela!' I am interrupted by Preston, who lives downstairs. He is in his sixties, slightly overweight, with thinning hair. Gay and single, he was in denial or in the closet for many years. He would say he is a seven out of ten, used to be an eight, but he grades me as a solid six.

Although attractive and always immaculately dressed, he drinks to excess, which is showing on his face. I hate to say he is an alcoholic, because he isn't lying in the street drunk, but he is one. His eyes are slightly glassy, the whites yellowing, and thread veins here and there mark his cheeks. His lips are purple-red instead of healthy pink. Preston would say he has been through the mill and had a fabulous time whilst there!

He has a million stories; some he repeats over and over, but others are so novel, so bizarre it makes me wonder whether he fabricates them—these amazing tales he never told me before. Sometimes, I wonder whether his camp, over-the-top bitchiness is pure show.

'Going shopping?' He peers at the list.

I hurriedly cover it up. 'Yes,' I lie, as I slip the list into the drawer with the cutlery. I get a teaspoon out and put the kettle on to boil. I do confide in Preston, but it's dangerous. He would happily tell my secrets to anyone, including strangers on the Internet, as long it was a gripping story.

I'm not subtle at hiding the list, but I can't tell him I'm writing a list of my enemies over tea and biscuits either. I change the subject, diverting to Preston's favourite subject—himself.

'I was wondering yesterday, why are you called Preston? It's a very modern name for a man your age. You should be called Billy or Jim.'

Preston's gaze swivels to the drawer. It's obvious I'm hiding something, but there is an opportunity for him to tell me a story, so he lets it pass. 'Well ... that's an interesting story.'

My plan has worked.

He sits as I lean against the counter, ready to make tea. Preston lets me proceed with my line of questioning.

'You're Scottish, like me. From round here, even, but it's not a local name. Let me guess ... you were conceived in Preston, Lancashire,' I joke. 'Is it like a Posh-and-Becks thing, like Brooklyn?'

He snorts. 'No, but you're on the right track.' Then he smirks and puts on a deadly serious expression.

'I'm named after Prestonpans.'

Prestonpans is a seaside town in East Lothian. It's like any seaside town in Scotland, a main street with shops, a mixture of older buildings and modern ones, a mining history. It is not glamorous in the slightest. I doubt every word. Surely Preston can see this on my face, but he continues.

'Let's say, Mum and Dad went on holiday to Seton Sands, and I came along nine months later.' Seton Sands is a caravan park near Prestonpans. 'They couldn't call me Seton Sands, could they? So Prestonpans was near enough ... Preston for short.' He looks smug now, as if he has told me something I did not know about him. I think he believes that makes him mysterious and interesting. It sounds ridiculous, and is no doubt a lie, but it's funny, so I laugh and shake my head.

This isn't enough for him. Preston got a hit off my laugh, and like any good addict, he needs another shot of attention. I concentrate on carrying the tea over to the table.

'I've a wee sister called Valencia.'

I've never heard him mention a sister before. I'm certain this is also a lie and she doesn't exist. I heard of a brother once.

It's too tempting for me not to join this double act. I am the straight man in this scenario, and certainly straighter than Preston, which is always the case.

'Oh. Did they come into some money and swap Seton Sands for Spain the year after?'

'No...' He waits. 'Mum saw it written on an orange crate and liked the sound of it.'

There we were: the punchline. It was light relief, so ridiculous that at least it took his mind of the list in the drawer.

He leaves me to my lie that I was going shopping. My cupboard is full, and so is my fridge. He must have seen this when I opened the fridge to get the milk. My list is not a shopping list, and he knows I am hiding something.

As soon as he leaves, I take the list from the drawer, gripping the special bucket list of those I'd love to whack with an inanimate object. I sing the 'Trolley Song' again, but this time, I change the words so the bell doesn't 'ding'. In my version, the spade does.

NINE

> I turned my Christmas tree into a gratitude tree. I planned to hang all my gratitudes on the branches in place of decorations. I invited others to hang theirs, too, and I showed my tree off on social media. I was praised for my positive attitude. I am 'So bold and inspirational!'

I vowed I wouldn't let a day go by without a fresh gratitude being hung on a branch. But it's absolutely sickening, and I struggle to a find a 'gratitude' every single day.

I think hard: I have a son, a kind of partner, a home, a campervan, and a gay man who lives downstairs and visits often—sometimes too often.

I can afford food, a bed, and a TV.

I feel selfish now for complaining, so that tree didn't help me one bit!

Brain cancer is like a selfish invasion of your mind. All cancer is selfish. It's hard not to be selfish in return.

As soon as I was diagnosed, I went home and started

counting days off in a calendar of death. It was mental torture, so I put a stop to it. I should make the days count instead.

What did I just write? A moment of positivity? Where did it come from? What sick sugary part of my brain decided on positivity today?

I am so inconsistent, but Brian loves this shit.

TEN

PRESTON LETS HIMSELF IN. I rarely lock the door. It's a hang-over habit from living on a Scottish Island for all those years. I should lock it; that would be sensible.

John is always saying, 'Lock your door!' but he has OCD—not for cleaning and organising, like me, but for checking locks, switches, and security. I joke I'm OCD, but it's simply cleaning. I like the mindless activity. It keeps my anxiety levels low.

I wish John was good at cleaning. I'd let him live with me then, but he stays in his own house on the far side of town. It's best, for both of us. I remind myself to take the toilet paper upstairs.

'Hiya. You coming out?' Preston asks. He is on a health kick because it's a new year. He does this every year.

I can't believe it's a new year already and I still haven't worked on my resolution from last year, which was to be able to touch my toes again. Time flies by. God, I sound like an old lady. But I'm getting on, right? Fifty is a year or so away.

I need to stretch more. I used to go to Pilates classes. I thought I was rubbish at it, but now I can't do half of the moves I could then.

My deterioration has been quick, I think. Then I recall it's three years since the Pilates class.

Still, I don't want to go out. During my time off work, I've done every walk in every direction in this whole area and every possible route and variation in between.

'Fine!' Preston snips and goes. He is on a mission, so he jogs off in his new trainers and tracksuit he bought himself for Christmas.

After he is gone, I go upstairs to tidy the bedrooms. Mine is on the second floor, and there is another floor with two bedrooms and two ensuites. Preston's flat is smaller still: two bedrooms, all on one floor. Upstairs, I prepare for another round of tedious sock-pairing.

I forgot to take toilet paper upstairs again! It's still on the bottom step, ready to go up. That is my thing: routine. Doesn't everyone do that? It's for upstairs, so I'll save up a bunch of things on the bottom step. When I'm going up, I'll take them all. Except then I'll step over them.

I peer out the window. I always fear leaving the handbrake off the van, so I check it hasn't idled into the middle of the car park since I last looked. The trees are bare, but the leaves will bud soon. I love spring. *Will I see another?*

Back downstairs, I open the fridge door. *We need milk.* I say *we,* but Callum, my son, is off to university. I'm alone in the flat, except for the cat and Callum's pet rat. I message Preston to get some milk while he's out. He texts back that he is going to the shop to buy sloe gin for us later, so he will get it then. *So much for his attempt at a health kick.*

He texts:
It gets you drunk, but not as fast.

Very funny, I reply.

The last time he drank sloe gin, he spent the second part of the night pretending to be Dorothy Squires. She was his uncle's favourite singer. No one remembers Dorothy Squires now. She's been forgotten, but she was a TV star for years. *Will they remember me?*

The day after the 'Dorothy show', Preston insisted he must have suffered an allergic reaction to the berries because he ended up with a terrible headache. I don't remember any anaphylaxis, only terrible lip-synching to YouTube videos.

I add another text:

Can you get me a Scotsman while you are there?

What kind would you like? Tall, dark and handsome, or wee and hairy?

Newspaper.

I can hear him tittering in my head. I lie on the couch and turn on the TV.

ELEVEN

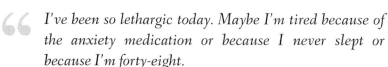

I've been so lethargic today. Maybe I'm tired because of the anxiety medication or because I never slept or because I'm forty-eight.

Maybe this is the proper menopause. It reminds me of the first weeks of my pregnancy. In fact, most of my pregnancy was like that, and the six months after giving birth, which I can't remember because I was so exhausted. But I'm not pregnant. I was tired like this before I learned of the last progression.

I don't like this tiredness. I want to be aware of everything. I want to be super-aware, tuned in to the point that I can feel the air moving in and out of my lungs. I can't be tired and groggy and miss a day. I need to be alert! I can't miss this last part of my life. But I'm so tired I haven't even the energy for rage, so at least that is a blessing.

I had to switch the telly off. I can't watch the news anymore—all the death and destruction and violence. Films, TV shows, or Callum's games with shoot-em-ups and killings are out of bounds too. Trivialising death as entertainment.

I'm reduced to comedies or rom-coms, although I know they're shit. Nightmares result otherwise, and I can't waste time on them.

I used to watch a girl on social media telling stories about serial killers, gory mysteries, and ghost stories, but it started to prey on me. I'd see things, faces. I'd turn over and still see them, appearing human or sometimes like bears or foxes. They weren't running at me or moving or talking; they were ... floating.

One night, I tried to take photograph or video on my phone; I was so convinced they were there. The following morning, the videos and images were of the wall or the ceiling, the bedside table and the lamp. The doctor said it was 'hypnagogic hallucinations' from stress and exhaustion mixed with medication. I didn't mention the booze to the doctor, but Google suggested that was part of it.

TWELVE

 I exist in a state of permanent anxiety. It constantly has its claws in me. Can you imagine your pet standing in the middle of the road with a lorry screeching right for it? That is my baseline.

Sometimes, I drown it out by keeping busy, by drinking alcohol. Maybe the grog caused Brian.

My modus operandi in anxious situations is self-harm with a side serving of suicidal ideation. I've controlled it with drugs and my understanding that this is how I am. This is me.

I self-harm every time I feel stressed, and then rage at myself for getting stressed and self-harming.

I used to hit myself in the head, always awfully hard and always on my hair area. It caused headaches and bumps, but no one could see them. It's the reason I've kept my thick hair long for years, apart from a short-lived crop that didn't suit my round face.

Maybe hitting my head caused Brian. I hope not.

I haven't hurt myself for years now, not since my ex Paddy. That tells you something about him.

Occasionally, I stick my nails in my arm to feel the instant pain that distracts me from a stressful situation. I've caused a lot of damage, a heavy weight I can just about carry, but what if I cracked and turned that pain against another?

My past reveals no evidence I could carry out violence. No harming of animals, for example.

Some boys from the university halls kicked a dead squirrel around the Botanic Gardens when I lived in Glasgow. I couldn't do that. I screamed at them till I cried. But that is how psychopaths act—they start small.

Still, I fear I might have it in me to lose control, to damage another human instead of just myself. To prove that I am, in truth, the awful person I think I am.

I TRY to choose healthy options for dinner, but then I give up. Lean meat and vegetables followed by a bottle of wine and some junk from the corner shop.

I need to use my time better. I check Facebook again; I see a meme about toilet paper panic-buying following a fuss on the news about snowy weather. It makes me smile. I write 'LOL', even though I didn't laugh out loud. This was not productive, but at least it will remind me about the toilet paper.

Here is another one, a life-affirming inspirational quote about smiling instead of self-loathing and spreading happiness. This is the positive stuff Brian likes. Sometimes, I think I can guess how he is feeling. He is a nice guy, Brian. He is the more positive part of my mind.

THIRTEEN

 I forgot the damn toilet paper again!

Anger overwhelmed me, of course. A lethal rage. I ripped the place apart, cursed, swore, punched mid-air, which is my level down from head-hitting. Then I picked up the gratitude tree and hauled the stupid thing into the bin, jamming it in as hard as I could. Stupid fucking thing was too big for the kitchen bin, which infuriated me even more.

I took a beta-blocker and spent some time tidying up the mess, hoovering up the smaller bits of tree. I know I need the beta-blockers because of the anxiety and my fury at the situation, but I always realise I need them too late.

They seem to be kicking in now. I should bag the bits of tree and take them down to the communal bins.

Anger wasn't part of my plan for dying gracefully, but it is here, nonetheless. At least I didn't get to the hitting myself stage today, as the tree took the brunt, but I am still shaken and wallowing in a pile of guilt for losing control. It's embarrassing, even though no one saw it.

It shows me what I am capable of.

I AM SETTLED in the kitchen with a cup of tea, editing my bucket list of enemies, when Preston arrives with the sloe gin. I see he started beforehand, and this is dessert. He is so drunk that his eyes are glassy and his bottom lip is hanging, leaving his mouth slightly open.

He drinks less often lately, as the doctors said he'll die of it. But when he does, he shows an incredible capacity for it. I'd be asleep or unconscious at half the amount he drinks, but, no, he is semi-lucid and still upright. He has had years of training. He'll have had a liquid starter and main course before this, which is for certain bottle number two. He thinks I don't know. I know. His liver knows too. It isn't up to it anymore.

'Hiya.' He introduces himself the usual way but more breathily. He has added a hand gesture, and he gives a half bow.

'Can you be even more camp, please?'

'Hiya,' he responds, even more flamboyantly. He practically sings it, and the bow is now at floor level. I wonder if he is ever going to rise. I wonder if it's all an act.

'What you doing?' he asks, as he heads to the kitchen with me following to get glasses.

'Writing a list of people I could murder.' I joke, tucking the list away in my diary.

He screams with laughter. 'For fuck's sake, I didn't know I lived below a psycho.'

He carries on preparing the drinks, getting the ice from the freezer. He would never miss out on the ice. He thinks that makes him sophisticated, a cut above the alcoholics stumbling in shop door-ways. He thinks making a drink without ice is common.

'That makes me like you even more. You are interesting, hen. I can't think of anything worse than being boring ... I'm not on the list, am I?' He howls and laughs, and then pulls a face.

'No,' I say, finally getting a word in.

'That's a relief. How you killing them off? Is it just a general stabbing spree or a mass shooting? And how many are we talking about here? Three, ten, twenty or are you going full Dr. Shipman?'

He is mid-monologue, so I know the question is rhetorical.

'When I think about it more, I know you aren't boring, but you aren't weird enough, and I don't know any middle-aged lady serial killers. The boy in the next block, you know the one, looks like his mother knitted him ...'

'Magnus.'

'Yeah. He could be a serial killer. It's the quiet ones who are the worst. He probably has a secret dungeon.'

'In the flats?' I interrupt. Preston carries on regardless.

'I'd get interviewed on *Sky News* after they found all the bodies.' He straightens up, puts his drink down, and pretends he is being interviewed. 'Well, he seemed such a nice chap, and he never bothered anybody. He lived with his mother ... I think she knitted his jumpers. He was always neat and tidy and polite. I would see him at the rubbish bins, and he would always let me go first. I never would have guessed.' He laughs loudly at his own humour before continuing. 'In hindsight, I was lucky not to end up one of the victims, really, turning my back on him at the bins. He could have tipped me in there anytime.'

We carry on drinking and head to the living room.

'Have you ever hated someone so much you could kill them?' I ask. I'm still angry from earlier. My ire has not gone away, and the gulps of alcohol have loosened my tongue. I wonder if I'm the only person who feels like this but keeps on without ever carrying it out.

'There are a few people I could happily help shuffle off into the pit of hell they deserve to end up in,' Preston answers with a smirk.

'Very dramatic.' I half-smile. 'Anyone in particular? I don't mean

someone who jumped a queue in front of you, but someone who hurt
you enough that you felt you could actually do the deed?'

Preston's smile leaves his face. 'I hate my brother enough.' His
voice changes to a more manly tone. 'He's a bit older than me. He
raped me when I was a bairn.' This was more than I was expecting, so
I let him go on. 'It was a regular occurrence, and then it would stop
for a while, so I thought that was it done with. I wanted to forget it,
but I was always scared of my bedroom door opening; then he'd come
back again. He tried it the last time when I was about 12, and I cut
him with a knife I'd stashed under the bed. He had to go to the
hospital for stitches.' He inhales deeply, sighs, and bites his cheek.

I say nothing. What can I say?

'So, then Mum and Dad knew. Maybe they knew already. Of
course, the main thing for them was they didn't want anyone else to
know. They said I could have killed him, as if that was the worst of it.
And if I said anything to anyone, they said they'd send me away. He
moved out, and that was how they fixed it.' He swallows a single sob
down with a swig of sloe gin.

'Did they disown him? I can't believe they never went to the
police.'

'No, they kept in contact with him. Got him accommodation
away from the house. They kept him away from me, at least. I never
saw him for years.'

'You've seen him since? Did you go looking for him?'

'No, I did not look for him,' he states indignantly. 'The bastard
showed up, though, at the hospital when my dad was dying, and I was
there. My mother forced me to make up with him, forgive him in
front of my dying dad so that he could leave in peace.'

I sit next to him and put my hand on his shoulder.

'I took one of those pocketknives in my coat pocket and had my
hand on it. I don't know how I managed not to stab him. I could have
stuck it in him ten times.' He mimes the action. 'I managed to say
those words, to forgive him, though, with my fingers crossed. I dinnae
forgive him or my bloody mother for sweeping it under the rug.'

I want to kill that arsehole who hurt Preston. I visualise it in my mind. Then, I know I could kill for real. If he were here right now, I'd stab him, no bother at all.

If I want to kill someone who has treated another person badly, I could certainly kill all those on the list who have been awful to me. They damaged my chances of a perfect life—a life that's been cut short. The title line from Bob Dylan's 'Don't Think Twice, It's All Right' comes into my head. I wouldn't think twice.

I bet the damage they did to me, the time they wasted for me, didn't even feature in their life, their time. I feel that if someone said the wrong word to me right now, that would be the end of him or her. Never mind about the consequences; I would bludgeon them to death. I don't like feeling this angry, and I can't show it in front of Preston. I should comfort him, but suddenly, it is all about me.

I excuse myself, leave him, and take a beta-blocker, which I swig down with a gin. I don't know if he knows what I'm doing, but I reckon he has seen me take them plenty of times before, so I don't care. I just need to get one in. Hopefully, he is too drunk or too upset to notice what I am poisoning myself with.

He goes to the toilet, and when he returns, I see he has washed his face and is calmer. He looks composed now, wary, like he gave too much away.

A gay best friend is supposed to be entertaining and fun, I think.

'Do you still see them, your mother and brother?' I venture.

'Oh yeah, we are all pals now.' He snorts. 'They come here some-times. I put on an amazing show, as if none of it ever happened. I told you I should be on the stage. I avoid them as much as possible, but they insist on keeping in touch. I speak to Mum on the phone, and then she visits and brings him. Well, he brings her in his clapped-out Cortina. He thinks he is cool because it's a classic car. She is old now, and she'll die soon. I tolerate him for her, just about,' he replies.

He has recovered from the earlier slip of the facade and somehow sobered up from some water to the face. I think back, but I've never seen them here. I must have been too preoccupied with work, cancer, or myself, to notice. I've certainly never been introduced.

'Are you okay?'

'Och, it was ages ago.' He brushes it off.

'Time passing ...' I nod. 'It helps.'

He sighs, and then replies, 'Yeah, but you know what they say ...' After a pause, he announces, 'As the saying goes: revenge is like custard.'

'Pardon?'

'Revenge is like custard—the well-known saying.' He sounds like an ancient sage imparting his wisdom.

'I've never heard of that.' I screw up my face.

'Of course you have. Revenge is like custard ... best served cold,' he says with the confidence of a barrister closing the case.

'I've heard revenge is a dish best served cold,' I reply, enunciating every word.

'That's it.' He is satisfied.

'That's not the same thing. Where is the custard?' I question.

'Well, custard is best served cold, like revenge.' He is getting exasperated with me now.

'So, you've changed it to revenge is like custard?' I ask.

'Yeah, best served cold.' He folds his arms.

'Is it, though?'

'Yeah, it's a well-known saying. You leave revenge till later and it's better.' He is beginning to smile, and the hand gestures are back.

'I mean custard? Is custard best served cold? Is it?' I am enjoying this now too.

'Yeah. Like in custard tarts and slices. I rest my case.' The case is closed yet again.

'Case reopened. Custard is not best served cold. How about warm on top of a sponge? I prefer it warm.'

He shakes his head at this, as if I am the strange one. As usual, I wonder how this conversation started, what it was all about, and whether Preston is entirely serious. Suddenly, and without any more alcohol, his posture changes. He seems giggly drunk again.

'Gimme your laptop.' He jumps up and types 'Dorothy Squires' into my search bar as fast as he can. Later, after he fetches my dressing gown and feather boa from the ensuite, I am treated to the camp version of *My Way* lip-synched out of time. He doesn't mention the irony of singing a song that starts with the end being near to a woman who is dying of cancer.

I own an ensuite, a chaise longue, a leopard-print nightdress and a gay BFF. I would have thought myself bloody wonderful if I'd seen into my future back in my university days. My twenty-year-old self would have been impressed, although a husband, more kids, and a detached house instead of a flat might have been better.

Preston falls asleep on the couch, so I put a blanket over him and a bowl nearby, just in case. I don't leave; he could choke on his own vomit. Some people do. Was it Mama Cass? Oh no, that was a sandwich. It was someone famous anyway. Some rock star or other.

I get the list from my diary.

FOURTEEN

These are the ones I'll kill. I always knew I was capable of it, so now is the time.

I am bound to get caught. Why wouldn't I? But I have seen enough TV detective dramas. They'd ask, 'What's the motive?' Most of my motives occurred years ago. Most of these people I have no contact with now. They are not in my circle. Actually, I do not even know where they live. I moved on and away from them. It would be very cold custard.

They are not even on my Facebook friends list. Facebook—there's a fine place to start—or Google. I suppose that might be evidence if they check my browser history. Why would they check that, though? And if they did, it might be too late.

But I don't want to get nicked halfway through the list, so I'll still need to be careful. I hate not finishing things. I'm the opposite of a procrastinator; I like to get on with it.

I am not disabled, and being symptom-free will help

me. I can get around to all the places I want to go. I'm off work because dying isn't the best career move, so I've plenty of time. I was encouraged to leave. I can go back anytime they said, knowing that would never happen.

Who doesn't want to go visit their past haunts and reminisce before they die? Visit old friends? See familiar places? A trip down memory lane. It's perfectly reasonable behaviour.

They'd need to work out a connection between the victims and me, and that is not clear to see. The single link between them is ... me. That thought makes me laugh out loud, not like a LOL on social media, a real belly laugh, like an evil genius. I should practice my baddie laugh!

I realise there are far too many names on my list. I'll need to whittle them down to who was the worst. Some on there are guilty of minor misdemeanours, so they deserve a lesser punishment. If it's too drawn out, I'll get caught and miss all the best ones.

I'll work it into sections based on who gets what as I go, but I need to give them their just deserts. Is it deserts or desserts? Is this a custard reference again?

It could be the sloe gin or the drugs, but I feel better already. My angry voice has been fed. I might even hang a new gratitude tree with a different name on every branch for every victim.

Victim? Not one of them! I was the victim. When I was scrolling through Facebook earlier, another meme made me smirk. I wrote LOL as a comment on it. It said, 'Sometimes, the only thing stopping me from murdering ... is the prison time.'

One thing I don't have is time. I cannot lose it, and it cannot stop me. I have no time left to lose.

FIFTEEN

THE NEXT DAY, I go browsing in the cancer charity shop. It's so bright and clean. Positive vibes positively bounce off the clean walls. The radio plays poppy tunes, and the white brightness of the lights is blinding. A breast cancer awareness pop-up poster adorns the window, and the counter holds a collection tin and some ribbons for sale.

It's Breast Cancer Day or Week/Month/Year—whatever. Its over-publicised advertising campaign desensitises breast cancer for me. It is all pink, pink, pink. Joyful, smiling survivor stories abound because who wants to hear about the cynical dead losers?

If breast cancer is pink, I wonder what colour brain cancer is? Brian is grey, like a brain. I must look up an image of the snail from *The Magic Roundabout,* and brain cancer ribbons.

Cancer is all about positivity, you know. Like if I put my mind to it, I could cure this tumour with a better attitude. But the Breast Cancer charity reminds us to please dig deep, as the cure is out there for those rational scientists to discover; clearly, positive thinking doesn't cut it in real life.

Still, I like a bargain. They sell new things, such as notebooks and journals, among the discarded clothes and bric-a-brac. I've returned to my stationery fetish. I spend some time deciding which one is best. I settle on a sparkly notebook. It's large and bulky, with plastic jewels sewn to the fabric cover. While there, I pick out more things I didn't know I needed.

I could go home, but what would I do? What chores are on my housework list? I mentally run through them, ticking off what I've already completed. All of it can wait. I've to sort out the socks again, remember to buy cat food, hoover the cat litter up, clean Callum's rat's cage out, and empty the bins. I remembered to empty the bins in the flat and place them at the door, but I forgot to take them down to the communal bins. It's the toilet paper scenario all over again.

I take the notebook to a nearby café and flip it open. I discretely smell it as I fold the pages flat. It's a pleasure to write in the first page of a new notebook; so many possibilities lie ahead.

I sort out the names from the Trump notepaper tucked in my diary and place them in order of appearance in my life, titling it 'Cold Custard'.

Life is too short to wait.

Cold Custard

- Miss Moleman
- The Man
- Tracey
- Julie
- Debbie
- Mark
- Elizabeth
- Tina
- Eric
- Brenda
- Simone
- Steve
- Kate

- Tom
- Chris
- Michael
- Douglas
- Paddy
- Linda
- Denise
- Mandy
- Sandra
- Gillian
- Barbara

Too many names—divide into sections.
This needs whittling down!
Too many kills, not enough time!

enjoy every moment.

First Section—School

- Miss Moleman
- The Man
- Tracey
- Julie
- Debbie

SIXTEEN

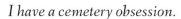

> I have a cemetery obsession.
>
> Cemeteries might be strange places to focus on for someone who is dying, but I've always liked them, and I am not put off now.
>
> I like to walk around them, looking at the headstones, pondering that everyone has their turn at life, and then it ends. They had their slot.
>
> Dying doesn't seem so unfair in a cemetery. Maybe this was my turn, and it was longer than some of the people lying in the graves were allocated. They've not been entirely forgotten, since others can read the details on their gravestones, but all those wee things that were important to them are gone.
>
> I enjoy wondering where they lived, what they loved, their talents. All forgotten. But all their worries are gone too.

I DECIDE TO TAKE A WALK. I won't bring Callum, who is home from university. He might like to go for a walk, but I worry he'll remember doing the walk with me when I die, and it could upset him.

The doctors say exercise will help with my mental health, and I'll get fitter, for all the good that will do me. John says it might help me sleep. We see each other rarely but speak on the phone each day. We are both too past it and damaged to deal with anything else.

I choose a trail walk with instructions on an app on my phone. It's a modern pastime, but it bothers me I can't even get back to nature without my phone. I use this type of trail because it gives me a purpose, and I struggle with walking for no reason. The trail app has clues or directions to each stage, where it tells you a bit of history then directs you to another point. I find out things I didn't know, which makes me happy. There I go killing the boredom, or, as Nana used to say, 'Getting the day shoved in.' Everyone is in such a hurry to get to the end.

I'm at a narrowing of the path and reading about the weir, where the water is raging after heavy rainfall. An iron apparatus here used to feed the mill lade, a kind of mini-canal from the river for the factories. It is now redundant, and the app asks walkers questions about it. I am required to note down the colour, so I stop to check it out. It's a matter of seconds before I click on 'Red' as my answer. I turn to leave.

'Fuck's sake. Folk are wanting to pass,' snaps a short man with white hair, wearing an anorak that looks too big for him. He marches past, angry with me for being in his way, although he managed to pass me without any trouble. His stride was perhaps slowed, and he didn't want to have to sidestep.

I feel a tightness in my chest and my face reddening. In seconds, my anger overwhelms my geek's interest in local history, and the calming feeling of being outside, learning, vanishes.

I could push him in the river. I walk away from him a little, imagining standing on the back of his neck while he is face-down, drowning. 'This all happened because you did not want to step to the side,' I would say.

I'm proud that all I actually managed to shout was, 'I think the words you are looking for are *Excuse me!*' I was late at shouting it, so I am not sure he heard, that or he was now embarrassed at harassing a woman for standing on a path he could negotiate without any trouble.

I know I'm a better person than him; I am angry too, but when I want to harm people, it is for good reason. I muse that the drowning I considered doesn't show me at my best. I don't want to waste my killings on someone like that. Not while there are Miss Molemans in the world.

SEVENTEEN

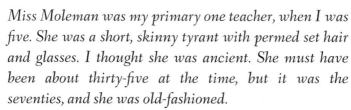

"Miss Moleman was my primary one teacher, when I was five. She was a short, skinny tyrant with permed set hair and glasses. I thought she was ancient. She must have been about thirty-five at the time, but it was the seventies, and she was old-fashioned.

She looked like something from wartime. I recall her being a grey and brown person. Her hair was grey-brown. Her clothes were grey-brown. I picture her now in sepia.

Her manner was stern and strict, and she frightened us all. She wore those half-glasses, and she'd peer over them like an eagle looking for prey. In her case, five-year-old children.

There was a Wendy house in the classroom, a water area with cups and apparatus, and a sandpit for playing. I never remember being allowed to play with them. They were there to show you what you would never be able to play with, for show at parents' evening. Our tiny five-year-old hands never touched them.

She had no patience with small children, or at least that's what the grip she had on my tiny wrist made me think. She was Miss Hannigan in Annie, minus the booze. Her aim in life was to be as vindictive and sadistic as she could on a daily basis.

She would walk up and down the classroom carrying a pointer. On her way to the back of the class, she noted anyone who moved. When she walked back, she would pick children at random, getting them to lean back from their desks and skelping them hard across their bare legs. You'd hear a swish, slap and whimper behind you, and wince, not knowing if you would be next.

I WALK UP the hill to the church and the cemetery. I stop at a gravestone that tells me of the father who died at forty years old; one daughter died at two years; a son at nine years. The second son drowned at sea at fourteen. The next two sons, named, strangely to me, the same as the first two sons, died in infancy.

A tree is growing out of the wall behind the headstone. There is no soil there that I can see, but it has found a way to live and grow regardless. The wife lived a long life, and the final daughter survived to eighty and was left on her own till 1978—around about the time I went to Sunday school in this church. At about the same time, I attended the school at the bottom of the hill.

I visit my great granny's grave. She is buried here with her daughter, who died aged fifty in 1980. I realise she lived a similar length of time as me, although at the time I thought she was old.

Down the steps from the cemetery, I walk to where I lived from the age of five through to seventeen. An estate agent would call it a 'Pleasant red-sandstone lower villa with bay windows.' It had a large living room, two decent-sized bedrooms, and a galley kitchen and bathroom. I peer in the window as I walk past.

I didn't notice it was cold until I was a teenager. It was normal to see ice on the inside of the windows as we were weighed down by the candlewick bedspreads. We had no central heating till later, and even then, we'd get dressed in front of the fire in the winter. I suffered from asthma, and the coal set me off, which was a shame. We got cheap coal because Dad was a miner. Sometimes, the electric heater was plugged in on cold winter days, and one, maybe two bars were fired up.

The primary school was at the end of the road that ran perpendicular to ours. Our house was opposite the junction. I would cross the road and walk straight on, and then turn right and I was there ...

'Good morning, Miss Moleman,' we would all sing. We'd get reprimanded for slouching or socks that needed to be pulled up. Every morning, she would inspect us like a terrifying, tiny sergeant major.

Every day and all day, she intimidated us. At the end of each day, she lined up whomsoever she decided was the naughtiest, got her ruler out and slapped their palms. She made a list as she went through the day. I never knew if I was due my turn.

The main culprits were always there. Russel and Carol were in for daily slaps, no matter what. Now and then, random children would be picked, sometimes for as little as not saying please and thank you. Lorna got rulered for swinging around the pole outside the toilets at the bottom of the stairs, and her sister for being left-handed. I think everyone got slapped with the ruler at some point.

Mrs. Kelso, who taught in the other primary one class opposite, looked like Hattie Jacques from the *Carry On* films and wore a giant smock dress that fell tent-like from her enormous bosom. I remember seeing Demis Roussos on TV and thinking they must have had the same tailor. Her hair was jet-black in short curls atop her jolly red face. I often wondered what it was like in her class. I hoped it was better than mine. I hoped to be moved across the corridor to safety.

At assembly one day, Kevin from Mrs. Kelso's class started running around the hall. Mrs. Kelso played the piano for assembly, so she carried on with 'All Things Bright and Beautiful' as he ran. A few teachers tried to grab him, but he was having fun dodging their rugby tackles. We carried on singing, watching until he got to the piano, where Mrs. Kelso stopped playing and tried to bar the way. She was too big an obstacle to swerve, so he grabbed a chair and threw it at her stomach. She barely flinched as it bounced off her belly. She chased him around the front of the hall, but he ducked under her arm and headed out the fire doors.

One side of the hall had huge floor to ceiling windows, so we could see Kevin run all the way to the gates with Mrs. Kelso in pursuit. He made it to the High Street before he got caught—it was the talk of the playground. It made me think Mrs. Kelso didn't quite have the grip on her class that Miss Moleman did. Miss Moleman never batted an eyelid throughout the whole incident. Her students would never dare behave like that.

Kevin was from the children's home nearby. Several orphan children and so-called 'bad boys and girls' attended our school. I don't know whether they were put in the home because they were bad or whether they ended up bad from being in there. Certainly, it was used as a threat in our house. 'You'll get put to the home if you don't behave.' I now know it was for children whose parents couldn't look after them.

There was an exposé of abuse in the home a while ago. Carol, who I think may have been abused, would show the boys her bare bum or knickers in exchange for sweets.

Another 'home pupil' was a girl called Tracey. She always looked dirty: grey-faced with a red, runny nose and chapped lips. Her hair was lank and greasy, stuck to her head in a bowl shape. My mum called it a pageboy style, but I sported a pageboy while hers was absolutely a bowl cut. She was skinny and her loose clothes, which looked borrowed or donated, hung from her frame. She was a regular for getting the ruler, but she was different from the rest of us. She didn't care. She would laugh in Miss Moleman's face.

One day, Miss Moleman refused to let Gordon go to the toilet. 'Learn to go at break times,' she commanded. He messed his trousers. She put him into the cupboard as punishment and got him to wear shorts from the lost property all day. He got the ruler for that, as if crying with embarrassment was not enough penance.

Diane and Gaynor spilt some egg off their sandwiches on the floor. She made them eat it off the floor like dogs, yelling, 'There are children in Africa who have no food. They'd be happy to eat this.'

Carol once arrived at school wearing wellies instead of the standard black shoes. Miss Moleman didn't consider the chaos at the home in getting all those children dressed in the morning. It must have been a case of first up was best dressed. She made her take them off, and all she was wearing underneath were socks with holes at the toes. This enraged Miss Moleman, who launched the blackboard duster across the class and hit Carol so hard that she fell to the ground and cut her head. Miss Moleman sent her to the school nurse with some story about a careless trip and fall. The nurse somehow swallowed the tale, even though the chalk dust in Carol's hair made her look like a grey-haired granny.

After that, Miss Moleman made her punishments less visible. The huge blackboard ruler across the shoulders was less noticeable, so it became the weapon of choice, although Russel got a pointed protractor stabbed in his back on occasion.

I walked out one day. I had asked to go to the toilet, and, surprisingly, she said yes. Perhaps after the Gordon incident, she couldn't cope with the hassle of the clean-up operation if she declined.

I went to the toilet, and then I walked on past the tiny coats hung on their pegs, which had pictures stuck there for the children who couldn't read their own names yet.

I had a choice.

I looked at the door of the classroom. I looked at the outer doors. I made the decision. Instead of turning left, back into the classroom, I carried on walking out the front double doors. I knew where the steps were. All I had to do was turn left and head up to the road to my house.

I marched up that road, wearing my blue painting pinny with the white trim on; I hadn't thought to take it off. I had never been on my own before. Five-year-olds don't get any independence.

I crossed the road at the junction—that was the most difficult part —and, once negotiated, I stood on my tiptoes and hit the knocker with the lion's face. My mother answered.

'I'm not going back there! I don't like it,' I said as I strolled past her into the hall and safety. My Auntie Elizabeth was in the living room. Mum had the special china out. After Mum recovered from the shock, she said, 'You can't just *not go back.*' She took me back down the road to the school.

Miss Moleman was horrified. I could see her talking to my Mum at the classroom door. She hadn't even noticed I was missing, which looked bad for her. She had let one escape, and she was apologising over and over. It was the first time I'd seen her anything less than fully in control.

I didn't get chosen for the ruler, although I had anticipated it. I had dared defy her and go out that room. I hadn't told Mum all the details, only that I didn't like school. All Mum recalls me saying was, 'They are trying to tell me what to do in there.' But Miss Moleman didn't know that. If I could walk once and tell Mum why I didn't want to be there, maybe I'd repeat it again ... with more detail.

Miss Moleman hated me and was unsure of me simultaneously. The day after my walkout, she stared right at me while Russel held the lid up at his desk next to mine. She continued to stare as she knocked that lid right down on his head. I knew she did it on purpose; her stare never left me. Russel got the ruler again that day ... for letting the desk lid fall on his head.

EIGHTEEN

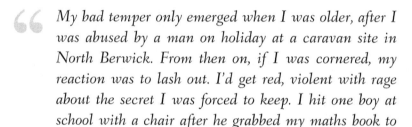

"*My bad temper only emerged when I was older, after I was abused by a man on holiday at a caravan site in North Berwick. From then on, if I was cornered, my reaction was to lash out. I'd get red, violent with rage about the secret I was forced to keep. I hit one boy at school with a chair after he grabbed my maths book to copy.*

My little sister was a bloody torment, as wee sisters often are. We would chase each other, rampaging around the house. I chased her one time, and in return, she chased me back. I ran into the bedroom and leaned against the door to shut it. It wouldn't shut. I kept shoving and shoving backwards. I thought she was winning, pushing against it to open it. Then I thought her foot was in the door. I looked down. No, her foot wasn't in the door. I looked up again. Her head was in the doorway. Laughing, I continued to jam her red-faced little head in there.

'Angela jammed my head in the door!'

I got in a lot of trouble for that, but who wedges a door open with their head?

On another occasion, I threw a scrubbing brush at her. And the time she cheated at swing ball, her punishment was my throwing a swing ball bat, like a knife thrower, and hitting her square between the eyes.

The Man was tall, and I guess around thirty years old. I was only eight or nine—everyone looks like an adult when you're that age. He could have been twenty or forty-five.

He was slim, wore brown cords and a tan polo-type shirt with a pointed collar. I don't know why I remember that detail. He was not handsome. He had a ginger mop of hair and a matching beard.

He was at the play park in the centre of the park, and he got me to sit on his knee while he let me steer the car. He put his hand where I didn't like, so I jumped off and he lifted my sister on. I pushed her off and sat on his knee to stop him doing the thing to her. He hurt me—in broad daylight. I guess everyone at the park thought he was my uncle or my dad.

'Open your legs.'

I tried, but what he was doing hurt, so I shut them tight again. He put me down. I was no use to him. I took my sister by the hand, and I ran.

Mum was busy, so I wasn't to interrupt. I did try to tell, but Mum shushed me, so I kept quiet. I didn't know the words to say to describe what had happened anyway, so I never told anyone till that one disastrous time later. That time when I'd invite questions as to why I didn't say so at the time. With that question comes the implication that it didn't happen at all. You are making it all up, a liar who wants attention.

That's where my relationship with food went wrong too. My parents liked to feed us, and I ate it all. All those cakes and sausage rolls I enjoyed consuming; they made me happy. Then my parents would say I was getting fat, so I added shame to the guilt and the belief I was a bad girl.

I took a toy figurine from the display at school because I wanted it, and no one would know. It was another secret, but one I had control over for a while. I eventually put it back. I felt like it was burning a hole in my pocket after teachers mentioned it at assembly. But having secrets could be exciting too.

AT SCHOOL, Tracey, from the home, also got violent as we got older.

She had two friends she was always with, Julie and Debbie. Julie and Debbie lived near the home. They were both Tracey's friends because it was too dangerous otherwise.

Julie was similar to Tracey, but a shorter, chubbier version. Mum always hoped we would become friends, as she knew Julie's mum from work. That never happened. Julie became Tracey's lackey, and Tracey was my enemy.

Debbie was pretty and blonde and neat. It gave Tracey some social standing to have Debbie on her team. Julie would join in with Tracey's bullying. Debbie was more passive, but if there were any telling to be done, Debbie would say she was there and saw nothing. She would even lie that the complainer was the bully. Debbie was the witness for the defence if anyone grassed on Tracey. It kept Debbie safe from bullying and it gave Tracey backup—a truly symbiotic relationship. Julie was too stupid to be devious. She simply enjoyed the thrill of power in a world where she would otherwise be the victim.

On our first day back at school, we had to do 'What we did on our holidays' talks. My parents inherited some money, so we went all the way to London and stayed in a lovely hotel in Kensington. It was one of the rare times we didn't visit Butlins or the caravan at North Berwick. I bought a canvas Harrods bag while I was there. I took it as my school bag and talked about my holiday in London. It's amazing what tiny things annoy people; something as little as going to London and buying a bag can drive someone crazy. Tracey wasn't happy about the situation at all.

'Who do you think you are? You think you are better than us.' She took my bag, threw it onto the ground, and kicked it. Julie egged her on. I was confused, but I know now she was envious. She had never been outside of Scotland. London must have seemed like the moon.

Tracey never liked me, and as two girls had already left the school because of her attacks, she found a new main target in me. I made her an enemy that day, as my secret had made me angry and all my rage came out. I grabbed the bag, weighty with all my school things in it, and spun it around and around like a hammer thrower. They watched, laughing at my angry little face. They didn't know what I was doing.

'You are stupid.'

I kept spinning faster and faster, their voices and laughter swimming in my ears.

'No wonder everyone hates you.'

I kept on spinning and spinning, and then I shifted my position so the path of the bag collided with Tracey's stupid, laughing, greasy face. She fell face down on the ground with no time to save herself. Julie ran away crying. I imagine she thought Tracey was dead.

After a few seconds of staring at her, bleeding from her face, hands, and knees on the grey gravel, I ran up the steps, turned left at the gate, and sprinted up the road home. I thought I had killed her.

You would think standing up to a bully was a positive move that might stop them. Instead, it made Tracey decide for certain that I was her 'Project Fear' from then on, with Julie and Debbie watching on. I hated them, too, for being part of it.

After one incident, in which Debbie and Tracey, with Debbie's younger sister, started calling me names, I pulled the younger girl's blazer off and threw it into a puddle in a fit of rage. I'd become the bully, according to Debbie, who got some older girls to pin me against the wall. She told the teachers I started it all by pulling off the blazer.

In a way, Debbie was worse than Tracey. She was the twisted, sly one—the one teachers thought would go far, perhaps even have her name in lights one day. The teachers loved her because she was pretty, perky, and clever. Not too clever, although her notebooks were the neatest. She would likely keep herself and her house nice, make a good wife, and marry well. It was the seventies; feminism hadn't quite hit the sticks around Edinburgh yet.

My parents took me out of school, as the bullying carried on. Others had already left. One girl went to the same school as me, another to a different school. I remember Mum sounding surprised at hearing that Tracey was picking on Miranda and Louise.

'Did you know?'

I was amazed she had no clue that Tracey had bullied me too? I guess I thought parents knew everything. Well, they don't ... not unless you tell them.

That's the power of secrets.

I walk home with that all in mind. As I pass the church, I remember Sunday school and all the Bible classes there. They didn't help. They were aimed at children who didn't have big secrets like mine. Their sins were minor. Anyway, you can't keep secrets from God.

Being told to repent for my sins every week was not the best thing for the guilt I carried. I still could not admit to anyone what had happened to me. I could never pray enough to take that away.

I feel it's been a productive day, assessing all these things as I walk. I'll go to the school again for more inspiration to decide how to deal with them. I'm pleased I remembered the cat food, and I'm ready now to go home and pair the socks, hoover up the cat litter. What was the last thing? Oh, yes! Take the bins out—the ones from the flat, and the ones from my childhood.

First Section—School

- Miss Moleman
- The Man
- Tracey
- Julie
- Debbie

Home, shop, bus, café

.

TWENTY

I STARE out the window into the car park. A frail old lady and a man of around seventy are getting into a car parked in one of the visitors' spaces. I've seen the car before, or maybe it is the man who seems familiar. The car is one from the 1970s or '80s. I guess it is a classic now.

The man is staring up at the flats, but not at mine. He isn't looking at me. I'm planting seeds in my planters on the balcony while spying on the car park. I wonder if I'll see the plants come up. This could be the last time I tend these boxes.

He doesn't help the old dear into the car; she is left to struggle into the passenger seat as he stands smoking, his free hand tucked in his jeans pocket. He wears a tan leather jacket, which is not appropriate for the weather. It's too cold for that—one of those cold but sunny March days that can con you into thinking it is spring, so best get the summer clothes out.

His shoulders are hunched, and he shifts from foot to foot. He is tall, not fat but not thin. I bet he was taller in his youth, but now he is a little stooped.

The most noticeable thing about him is that, despite his age, he has the most striking red hair, the reddest I have ever seen. It almost matches his face; perhaps he is a heavy drinker. After some time, he and the lady leave in the car.

I mention the pair to Preston, who has swanned in. He looks out the window at where they were.

'That's them, the Addams Family,' he states, as he turns and sits at the kitchen table. I realise I have been looking at his mother and his brother. I look back to where they were, as if I'd get a second look at them. I consider asking where the mythical sister Valencia is, but as I turn, I see Preston's serious expression, so instead I say, 'Are they that awful now? They look normal.'

'The fucking Waltons we ain't, remember,' he snaps. I nod. I remind him about the conversation where he wanted revenge on them, and I wonder if anything untoward happened today, although they drove away apparently unscathed.

'I'll wait. Something will happen to him and I'll see my own day.' He sulks, but then he livens up with a wicked grin and spins around to face me.

'I put a curse on him.'

'A curse?' I raise my eyebrows. Again, this is the first time I have heard this from him.

'Yeah, I'm part Irish, from travelling folk, we can curse people, and I cursed him. One day, a house will fall on him. One day, I'll see it.'

'What would you do if it didn't ...? What if you couldn't wait, or you waited so long you thought it would never happen? Would you get revenge then?'

'Cold custard. I'll wait. Or crème brûlée if you prefer. Yes, crème brûlée. I am posher than a custard slice.'

He's not got the killer instinct like me. It keeps creeping into my head. I know I am capable. I know I am bad enough.

'I'm going to the home,' I announce.

'My home?' he asks. It's not *his* home. He works in the kitchen at the old folks' home and cooks for the residents. He is a better chef than is required for there, but he likes the hours with no late nights. It's local, and there are never any complaints from the customers. Also, he used to work for Debbie in the High Street, and he told me her place wasn't clean.

'What? Are you getting put in there? Well, you are getting on right enough,' he titters.

'No, I'm visiting someone. I might see if I can volunteer for befriending maybe.'

'Oh yeah, we get folk in doing that. Who you visiting?' he asks. 'I know them all.'

'My primary schoolteacher, Miss Moleman.'

'Moleman ... Moleman,' he muses. '... Agnes?'

'I dunno her Christian name' I shrug. It never occurred to me that she had one.

'Aye, it will be. Agnes.'

'Is she all right? She must be ancient.'

'Nah! She's gaga. God, take me out and shoot me if I ever end up like that. She just sits in a chair, looking out the window, drooling. You know I'm a fabulous cook, yeah? I make amazing meals for them. One day, I even did that thing where you go round the plate with the napkin to pick up any stray splashes of gravy before presenting it to Madame. Presentation is everything, right? I laid it down with a "tada!"'

'And?'

'Then Agnes put her face right in it. Face palmed the tatties on the plate. Neednae have bothered.' He is laughing at the memory. 'Bloody hell, all my effort for nothing. Maria and me were pishing ourselves. They don't treat them right, you know. That bitch Jackie who runs it is just after the money. They aren't right to the old dears. Well, some of them aren't. Maria and Lesley are fine. I mean, have you seen the place? It's like Dracula's mansion.'

It is a Victorian building at the far end of town. 'It's a right draughty old joint. They freeze their bones in there, but the sons and daughters are quite happy cos they can drive up the big driveway and tell all their pals they've put the oldies in a stately home. It relieves their guilt. It's a bloody house of horrors. The stories I could tell ... but it's a wage.' He pauses for breath. 'I think Agnes is in the extension at the back. I tell you, when I get to that stage, I'm taking a bottle of vodka up the hills and ending it. They'll find me later, but I'll be frozen by then, and I'll have been off my head with drink, so I'll be none the wiser.

'Better take two bottles just in case,' I joke.

He thinks this is a scream. He has forgotten I won't get old.

I am quite enamoured by my situation now. I see it as an advantage, after his description of the alternative.

TWENTY-ONE

"The snail from The Magic Roundabout *has a pink human face, but his body is yellow. I looked it up. The brain cancer charity ribbon has the colour grey. These are my fun facts of the day.*

I think my Brian is grey, so some of that fits. His sunny personality gives him a yellow jumper in my mind, like the snail.

I think about breast cancer victims. Do they have lists too? Often, I think people are being boring and mundane, their minds full of white noise, and then you find out things; skeletons in the closet you never knew. Affairs taking place, or people so sad they take their own lives, and you had no idea.

Then there are times you realise there is nothing of the sort going on. All the people are just plodding along; they have no mission as far as I know. The boring people are thinking of buying The Sun *and a bottle of coke from the store, how to put on makeup well, or what the football scores are.*

I CLEAN THE HOUSE, my therapy. I set my robot hoover and my automatic cat toilet on the go. I run out of chores. Callum is away again, so I've less tidying and cleaning to do. I go for a walk, around town this time. I pass it all the time, but I decide to take a closer look at the school. Again, this gives me a bit of a thrill. I am up to something, and no one knows. I have another secret.

I walk boldly, as there is nothing more suspicious than someone creeping about. I have a notepad with me, as I always like to write. It opens doors, more so if you carry a clipboard, which can look official if you stride purposefully so no one questions you.

I try the gates at the High Street side, at the back of the school. They are locked, so I walk to the other larger back gate, where cars can enter. It's wide open.

They put on events outside school hours, like night schools and rehearsals for the local 'am-dram', so the car park needs to be open. The janitor knows me from such things, so if he is here, I could say I'm sketching, or I could admit I'm looking for a wee reminisce. I might say I left my gloves in the hall. I think this is the best idea. He won't find them, as they are in my pocket, but I feel covered for roaming about a school playground.

I try to get around to the front door, but both side gates are shut and the main one was locked when I passed earlier. The classroom I was in is visible from the side, where there is now a fenced-off garden area. The garden didn't have a fence around it when I was there; maybe we didn't try to escape as often, or the fear of children getting stolen wasn't considered.

To me, it looks exactly the same inside. I suppose it's more modern, but how 'more modern' can you make a square room with tiny desks and chairs? Some things don't change.

It brings back a time I made up a story about boys bullying me when I got really upset at dropping a puzzle toy down a drain. The adults questioned me about my crying, said it couldn't just be about this toy because I was too big a girl to be making such a fuss. I didn't even know why I cried like that at the time. Looking back, I was worried about my secret, so all my emotions poured out. When they offered up the suggestion that maybe boys were bullying me, I agreed. I was made to name names. I made up a story to stop the questioning.

Back at school, the boys were in trouble for what I said. They didn't speak to me after that. They didn't know why I lied that they had bullied me, but it was better than telling my truth. I feel sick with anxiety and guilt about it, even now. I did something bad to hide my guilt over something bad someone else had done to me. Evil leads to evil ... maybe the man who swore at me the river crossing had had a rotten day, so he wanted to hurt me. And then, of course, I wanted to drown him. These things just seem to escalate.

I head out the big gate and along the road behind the High Street and wander past Debbie's café. It's actually called 'Debbie's.' The teachers said she'd have her name in lights, and it's up there now in Medium Density Fibreboard. Queen Bees of anywhere never have any reason to change their location. They thought she'd go far. You could throw a stone from the school assembly hall and hit the back door of Debbie's café. She didn't go that far at all.

It's the messiest backyard of all the shops in the High Street. Preston says her kitchen wasn't clean. Based on the yard outside, with the bins overflowing, I believe him. The back door is open, and I peer in. I think I see her, but I'm quite far away as the car park at the back is large and full of cars. I see one with a personal number plate, DR. She's there.

I walk through the pend, or vennel, or whatever you call this passageway to the High Street to her café front door. I go on in and order a cup of Earl Grey. I daren't eat anything, and I don't want to give her much of my cash. A child serves me, around sixteen years old, and Debbie does not show her face. She wouldn't lower herself to mingle with the public.

I stay for a while and check out the toilets. Dirty grey nets adorn the frosted window. The ledge is home to a couple of dead flies and a dried-up air freshener that hasn't been replaced in quite some time. It's clear the contents of the crusty bottle of bleach in the corner are thrown about a bit at the end of the day, but that's about all. I take a plastic container out of my bag.

Callum has a pet rat called Rats Domino—he is white with a couple of black spots on his back. I saved up Rats Domino's droppings over the last three days. I place some behind the nets and in the corners. Back at my seat, I lay more under the table, against the skirting in that corner part the mop misses. As soon as I'm out of there, I make a phone call to the Council's Environmental Health.

TWENTY-TWO

I can't find The Man, my abuser. It's hard to guess his age, as I was so young. Forty years ago, Miss Moleman looked about eighty, yet she lives on.

He was already a man in the 1970s—a man with a ginger beard and brown flared cords. Who would know who he was?

Perhaps he lived there the whole time, although he was more likely on holiday. It was a holiday resort. Even if I said anything a week after, he would have been gone.

Sometimes when I see convicted paedophiles on TV, I wonder whether that was The Man years later. I wonder if he was married, whether he abused his own children. Maybe I caused more girls to end up abused because I didn't say anything. My head hurts when I think of that, and it makes me pull my hair, just to feel the hurt a bit.

I can't fix this now. It's too late. I couldn't even all that time ago. For years, it was a little niggle in my brain. For years, I felt sick.

Later, it faded, more like a cine film flickering in my mind. It's an old, orange-tinted film happening in my head right now. I can't remember what I did last week, but that memory never ever leaves entirely.

THE NEXT DAY, I visit the cut-price supermarket near where John lives. I'll buy some groceries, some booze for Preston, and cat food. It is not an upmarket store, but one that's a bit of a mess and they serve you in a hurry.

I go in, and she is there, on the checkout wearing a tabard. The back of her greasy head is the giveaway.

It's strange how people look different to their younger self. If you didn't know them when they were younger, you might not notice. But when you knew them as a young person, you still see that young person staring out at you with familiar eyes. The checkout operator's eyes stare at me in faint recognition when she turns my way. I see her name badge: 'TRACEY—Here to Serve.'

I'd tried to find her on Facebook before, but she evaded me. Women are harder to find because they get married. I drew a blank for a while, until I called Louise, who was at school with us. We reminisced about school days, and she brought Tracey up unbidden.

'Remember Tracey? She was a bloody nutter. I saw her a few years ago. She was working in the corner shop. Can you believe it? That was after she got out of jail. Attacked her husband in the kitchen one night. He could have died! She had a list of previous. It was one assault too many, so they threw her in the clink.'

This seemed more like the Tracey we knew and did not love. I searched birth and marriage records and discovered she had married not once but twice. I guess attempted murder is reason enough for divorce. Two people married Tracey! She received at least two proposals ... *Well done, Trace.* I only managed one.

I found her then, on Facebook under her second married name, living in a poor area with an old man. Her page revealed little of note. No holidays to London, for example.

Did she suffer enough in her childhood and later life? She had no fancy clothes, no money, no holidays—no wonder she was mad. I started to pity her and wonder what made her so angry so young. She was in a home that was notorious for abuse. Being left there alone must have been hard.

My empathy is becoming problematic.

I swan around the supermarket with a basket, picking the odd thing up. There is no sloe gin, so I get the plain stuff. I made a special effort today, wearing high heels, lipstick, my best bag, and sunglasses. I am completely out of place. I head to the checkout area and stare at her the whole time. *Hell, Tracey, not so clever now.*

I pretend I don't remember her. I am starting to sweat under my posh coat.

'Do you want me to bag?' she says before I interrupt.

'Bag it.' I let her bag my shopping. I help with this sort of thing, as a rule. I don't agree with being rude to service staff. This time, I do not aid her but instead play with my phone. When the transaction is complete, I lean in to get my receipt.

'Interesting shop—no Harrods, though, is it?' I whisper to her and perform a Preston-style flourish with my hand. I spin to go. I do not look back, but I can see her reflection in the window, not serving the next person in the queue but staring at me.

I'm done with her. Her life is suffering enough.

I put my shopping in the van to save me going up to the flat and to avoid meeting Preston on the stairs, which would hold me up. As I pass the bus stop on the way to the home, I recall I saw Julie here ten years ago without Tracey. We were waiting for a bus. She had peered at me.

'Do I know you?' she had asked, tentatively.

'Yeah.' I raised my brows but smiled a toothless smile, lips clenched.

'Did you go to the school ... ?' She gestured in the general direction, and her voice trailed off. I could tell she was recalling the things she did. Her bus came to save her; she looked at the ground until it was time for her to get on.

'Nice seeing you,' I shouted after her. She didn't answer.

After our chance meeting, I had seen Julie at the bus stop again the following day. She saw me coming and dashed around the corner. She missed her bus through shame.

Today, a quick shove under the Number 26 could sort Julie out, but she's not here where I saw her years ago, way before Brian and the list. Julie is scared of me now, because she isn't in Tracey's gang anymore. That is enough for me, so I don't seek her out now.

TWENTY-THREE

“ *People can so easily fall in front of buses; they come so near the kerbs, which are trip hazards. I mean, an ankle could buckle, and before you know it, you're under the wheel. I know someone who got hit by a bus wing mirror while walking along North Bridge. The bus came so close to the kerb it clipped them and they landed in a shop doorway.*

But that's no way to off Miss Moleman. She's in a care home. I wonder how to deal with her. It's unkind to abuse old ladies, like in that undercover documentary where lovely old dears were slapped about by staff. Not all old ladies are lovely, though. Some are horrible, nasty old ladies because they were horrible, nasty young ladies.

I don't know why Miss Moleman was awful and targeted tiny children. She never married or had any children of her own. Was she bitter about that? She was a vile person. I'm planning murders, and I still don't think I'm as evil as her.

I was a nice child. Abused at eight, raped at eighteen, I guess I've Post Traumatic Stress Disorder.

Cancer at forty-two—I forgot the cancer thing! I wonder what I have done to cause it. The 'Where does it come from?' question. With brain cancer, it's all in your head, in your mind. Have my terrible thoughts caused it? Is Brian a manifestation of my guilt and my anger? Has he been fed on shame and fury?

I don't know what I'm thinking. There are too many thoughts. It is making my head sore.

I WALK AROUND to the nursing home. I'd rung last week, said I was an old pupil who'd like to see Miss Moleman and asked about volunteering as a befriender. I've not got time to waste doing 'befriending' for real, but it gets me in the door. Lorna had told me Miss Moleman lived there. She'd seen her as a client in the hair-dressers and washed her hair in hotter than usual water. 'You should have done more damage with the scissors,' I'd joked.

On my visit, wandering the corridors after the carer, I toy with leaving the fire door open to aid me, but too many people can see you come and go in a corridor, and they could use CCTV, so I rule it out. Miss Moleman's room is in the less-glamorous annex of the mansion, the modern extension part on the ground floor at the back, which they don't put on the cover of the brochure.

'You'll not get much out of her,' says Lesley, the carer, as she marches down the hall. Lesley is a grown woman with the voice of an eight-year-old. She is very pleasant, but I'm glad I don't have to spend a lot of time with her.

'I'll chat and maybe play music. That sometimes helps dementia, doesn't it?' I reply.

'Aw, that's a lovely idea. Here she is. Hiya, Agnes. Somebody to see you.'

She sits hunched in a chair that faces the window. She gives a grunt or a sigh now and then but has no words. I don't sit down.

Incontinence pads are packed on the bedside table. Miss Moleman pees herself, like Gordon did. I feel like shoving her in the cupboard.

A tea trolley with a tray of half-eaten food is pushed to one side of the bed. Lesley never thought to take it away. I can see bits of her lunch she has dropped on the floor, some crumbs on her top. She would have made me eat that off the floor. Here she is spilling her food all over herself! She is like a child now, and no one has punished her like she did all those children. She doesn't say please or thank you, and her stocking is crumpled. Even her cardigan buttons aren't done up properly. We'd have been told off for that too.

I glance around. There is no CCTV in the room. I tut at her mess and take out the ruler I bought at the charity shop. I suppose it's vintage or retro; it is a wooden ruler, not one of those plastic, shatter-proof ones. She didn't use a plastic ruler. Hers was one like this. I flick it down hard on the back of her hand. Miss Moleman doesn't even flinch. After a while, her eyes move to mine. I place the ruler in her hand, and she grips the familiar object.

I open the window and wedge some card in, so the latch is off. The card pokes out to the outside, but you can't see it from inside. I pull the curtain over a little to cover the slightly cracked open window. I hope no one sees it is open and locks it later.

'That's me away, Lesley,' I call on my way out.

'Okay. Was she okay? Here's your leaflets,' she says in her Minnie Mouse voice.

'Oh, thanks.' I don't answer her question. I almost forgot the befriending. I take the leaflets off her. 'Thanks for that. See you again,' I lie.

'Shame for her.'

'Aye, shame.'

I RETURN in the wee hours. A path skirts the back wall of the estate, and there is a rotten door I can push open to avoid another walk up the driveway. Miss Moleman's jarred open window is practically at the wall. They extended the building so far back towards the wall that I need to breathe in to shimmy along the tiny space that's left.

The card I placed hanging out shows me I am at the correct window. I pull the window open. I can't get up there without a huge amount of effort, but the wall helps me haul myself up. I am cautious about not making a lot of noise. All the balancing and the effort and the keeping in the noises makes me feel red in the face, and I feel a sharp pain in my leg where I sit on the thin outer rim of the window frame, but I don't cry out. I keep quiet. I lower myself down. I shut the window for the cold.

She is lying still. A pillow over her head for four minutes does it. It seems an interminable time as I hold it there, but I count the seconds to myself. When I pull it away, it's hard to tell if anything has changed. I thought of choking her with powdered chalk, but that wouldn't be found in a nursing home. I don't want it to look suspicious. I toyed with the idea of ramming that wooden ruler down her throat too. I spot it on the bedside table and put it in her hand again, leaving it there. I won't leave any fingerprints, as I'm wearing gloves.

'Good morning, Miss Moleman,' I sing-song. I stand up straight. I don't slouch. My socks are up. I bid her farewell.

It's easier on the way out. I'm up and over in no time. I decide not to bother with the door and go straight to sitting on the wall. I nudge the window shut as best I can with my foot. I can't lock it from the outside, so I hope the latch falls down. I don't leave the card in because people might wonder why it was there. If the window blows ajar, maybe the staff will blame each other for leaving it open.

I stumble onto the grass. Over the wall, the path turns into a wooded area around the football pitches. I prefer being hidden in the trees to being out the open playing fields, so I walk the path over the burn and then on half a mile to exit at the main road. I've walked it many times and it's always quiet, and it's 5.30am. I suppose I'd look suspicious if I were seen here now, but it's even too early for dog walkers. I'll shout at an imaginary pooch if anyone stumbles across me.

It's starting to get light already. I like the light mornings and evenings now. I used to like cosy darkness, coal fires, port and cheese, and snow outside. I get a headache with port ... well, that time Preston and I drank a bottle each. When I get home, my pulse is still racing from the brisk walk.

TWENTY-FOUR

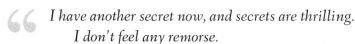

"   *I have another secret now, and secrets are thrilling.*

I don't feel any remorse.

I must be a psychopath. Would I know if I were a psychopath?

I'm a bit scared, though, or maybe it's excitement. Do psychopaths get excited or scared? Maybe I'm just scared I'll get caught and be unable to finish the list.

I don't care that she is dead. I thought I'd feel more, but I seem to possess no empathy. I'm glad about that, or how would I go on with the list?

I'm in control. I'll cross out when each section is done in my sparkly journal. I'll score out some as impossible or surplus to requirements in the death list. I could work it like a competition. Round one of the Death Factor: Miss Moleman, you were the winner of Section 1.

First Section—School

- ~~Miss Moleman~~
- ~~The Man~~
- ~~Tracey~~
- ~~Julie~~
- ~~Debbie~~

Home, shop, bus, café

TWENTY-FIVE

A POLICE CAR DRIVES BY, and the siren rings out for a few seconds, perhaps accidentally, as little traffic is on the road. The noise keeps blaring in my ears. But it is not sirens after all. The noise gets higher and higher pitched, until it is so high and so loud that it hurts my eardrums.

I can't breathe, like something's stuck in my throat. My heart is pounding so hard it's making my entire chest thump. I can hear my own muffled sobs and heavy breathing at a distance, almost like they're coming from another room or not really happening.

My head hurts again. I can hear something else too. *Is it the blood pumping through my veins?* I look down at my hands, sweating and shaking, jerking inches back and forth.

I get dizzier, my vision starts to blur, all of the sounds are echoing like I'm underwater in the swimming pool. It's like I am drowning and can't quite gasp the air back in when I reach the surface. My legs give way, and I feel the cold, hard, tiled floor of the kitchen before all goes black.

When I come to, I raise myself to sitting, leaning against the wall.

I *am* the terrible person I always knew I was. I thought I was capable of this, and now I have confirmed it. I am a monster!

I start slapping my head, punching it with my clenched fists over and over until I'm tired out. I reason that the beating was all I deserved. I needed a decent reboot to knock some sense into my head. I only punch where my hair is thick. I always hit where it isn't seen; I learnt that from Miss Moleman.

Second Section—University

- Mark
- Elizabeth
- Tina

TWENTY-SIX

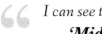

I can see the headlines...

'Middle-Aged Woman Hates Chocolate!'

It's as if I hated prosecco. (I like prosecco, however.) I don't like Easter eggs. The shops are full of them right now, and cute bunnies and spring flowers.

The Church has more of a presence at this time of year. I see they are happy to promote themselves without fear of offending or accusations of 'ramming religion down my throat'. People tolerate religion on the big holidays, especially when chocolate is involved.

I wonder how many Easters I have left. It makes me think of Easter Road and Tynecastle, where I used to get lifted over the turnstile to see Celtic play Hibs and Hearts—even up to the age of thirteen when I was a fatty and it took both my father and grandfather to do it. Even then, we were at the wrong end of the ground, so I had to keep my mouth shut.

Celtic was our team, mainly because my dad's side of the family was Irish Catholic. I was brought up

Protestant. I went to a girls' school after I left primary, which made me a bit boy mad, or Disney Princess boy mad. I developed romantic illusions. I'd read Across the Barricades *and had a romantic notion of sectarian division overcome with love, even though sectarian conflict was nothing I'd experienced. I thought I'd meet a lovely prince at university and live happily ever after. I was such an idiot.*

TWENTY-SEVEN

I'M WEARING the Glasgow University hoodie I got on a recent trip back. It took me a while to like Glasgow again, but I'm okay with it now.

I went to Glasgow University because it hosted the course I wanted, and I liked Celtic Football Club. In Glasgow, I could go to the football for real with my scarf on, and I could shout as loud as I wanted. I was taking the feminist, career-woman thing only so far. My going to university was a positive for my family because they hoped I might at least marry a doctor or a lawyer. It made university a better sell, as they wanted me to get a job in the bank to earn money, rather than just swanning around Glasgow.

I had some enjoyable times swanning around Glasgow, though— the time of my life, although I didn't know it then. It's a pity it wasn't as perfect as it could have been. *He* spoiled my memory.

I turned up at Fresher's Week wearing a Celtic tracksuit. I looked like a ned amongst all the cool students; what an idiot I was. I took off the jacket part and pulled the black top I was wearing over the bottoms, so I wasn't a walking advert for a football team.

Everyone was grouped with friends already. I spotted one girl from my school, and I was relieved to see her, but she looked less than impressed to see me. She spoke for a short time but said goodbye as soon as her friends asked her to join them.

I joined the Celtic Supporters Club for a pound and hung around trying to talk to the two boys behind the table. They said to meet them in the beer bar on Wednesday, and we'd go to the game from there. It was clear I was to leave the table and go elsewhere. I was the single girl in the group when we met in the bar to go to the game. It was obvious they didn't want to know me.

I trailed behind as they marched along the road to the ground that dark, rainy Wednesday. I went on my own after that. It was an adventure on the train and a walk following the crowds, as I'd forgotten the way. At the game, hot steaming piss from men behind me would trickle down the steps onto my trainers. I couldn't dodge it when the stadium was packed. 'Macaroons, Mars Bars.' An old guy would walk around selling knock-off sweets. How he made his way among the masses I wasn't sure, but he covered the whole area.

Some games were quiet, but sometimes it was so crowded I got lifted off my feet and carried to the front. It was both thrilling and terrifying after the disasters I'd seen on TV. I'd get chips on the way home and odd stares from the students when I returned to halls in my full Celtic regalia. I never admitted to having been on my own all day. I made out I had lots of friends outside halls—to make myself interesting.

After my departure from the Celtic table, I had joined the Revolutionary Communist Party. I joined because the guy behind the table looked as lonely as I was, and he was cute. He took me for a coffee and talked intensely about abortion rights and social justice. I was glad of the company, so I nodded, listened. A couple sat at the table behind heard me tell the lad where my halls were. Sensing that I needed saving, they butted in to say that was where they were going and did I want to help them find it? I jumped at the chance. They rescued me from the imminent revolutionary uprising, and we found our rooms. I never went to that chap's meetings, and I didn't see him again, but at least he got my pound for joining up.

As we passed, my new pals and I joined the Women's Queen Margaret Union. It took men by then, too, and it was where the Goths, the better music and bands were. On occasion, we would go the Glasgow University Union, or GUU, too. It was previously a men's union, but it now took girls and allowed us a cheap final venue for pub crawls. It was popular with rugby types. I met *him* there.

I was in first year, and he was a PhD student. I was eighteen years old and he was twenty-six. We'd gone from the beer bar to the night-club part of the GUU, and he asked me to dance to The Stone Roses or Goodbye Mr. Mackenzie or something. It might even have been Betty Boo, for all I knew.

He was slim, wearing jeans and a navy suit jacket. His friends were a bantering gang of boisterous, good-looking lads. They made the boys at the halls seem exactly that: boys. These were cool Glaswegian men.

Mark was clearly the leader of the gang, and the funniest. The others fell about laughing when he joked. I wanted to join his gang. They were like the imaginary friends I had made up for my hall pals, but for real.

Feeling too drunk, I abandoned my hall cronies and stood outside in the fresh air. I was going to leave and walk home alone, but I felt a bit queasy, so I was sitting on the step outside when Mark's gang appeared and joined me. They thought I was upset. I wasn't—it was the fresh air hitting me after the sweaty club, and I needed a moment before I headed up the hill. They asked me to their flat to hang out with them. I was a bit wary, but alcohol made the decision for me.

As I walked with them, they chatted and made me the centre of attention. I was one girl in a gang of four men, so I suppose they were fighting over me. We sat in their kitchen, and I made an attentive audience for their chatter, full of in-jokes that I became party to. I was tired, so they suggested I stayed. They kindly didn't think I should walk home in the middle of the night. Or perhaps they were too lazy to walk me all the way to the halls. I was directed to a spare room belonging to their friend Keith, who was away seeing his girlfriend for the weekend. A photo of them smiling together stood on the bedside table.

Mark, cigarette in hand, followed me into the room and sat for a while holding my hand. He lay down and curled into my back. I was aware of Craig coming in, saying, 'What's going on here, then?' Mark laughed, jumped up, and chased him out. He came back and stood looking at me for a while, and then he kissed me on the cheek and left.

In the morning, I woke up looking at an unfamiliar ceiling. Where the hell was this? I gingerly squinted about the room. Glasgow Rangers Football Club paraphernalia was everywhere: a red, white, and blue scarf hung from a wardrobe door, a pendant on the wall, a shirt over a chair. I was bewildered. I checked under the covers—still fully dressed. Then I saw Keith and his girlfriend smiling at me from the photo by the bed.

I plodded about the room, checking his things, while I pieced together how I had got here. I didn't know what time it was, and I wondered whether I should leave or shout out. I got a glass of water from the kitchen and decided to go when Mark and Craig, both dressed in T-shirts and boxers, came in.

'I'm just worried about not telling anyone where I went last night,' I said.

'Just tell them you went to hang out with friends,' Mark suggested, unconcerned. I liked that idea. I now knew cool guy friends—Mark, Joe, Craig, and David. I was in the gang. Mark asked for my number and kissed me at the front door.

I walked home in a daze of excitement. I'd had an adventure and made friends. The cool 'top guy' liked me.

Mark called me on the hall phone a week later. The loudspeaker announced, 'Phone call for Angela.' He waited a few minutes for me to walk down from the second floor at the back of the huge building to the foyer.

'Can I come round?' he said.

Why not? I thought. He followed me up the stairs to my room, all the way through the common room, the annex stairs, and along the corridor to my room, second from the end. I couldn't think what to say without alcohol, so we walked in silence, him behind me. I could see others looking at him. My mature, potential boyfriend paraded in front of all those silly teenagers.

We met Paulina on the way along the corridor.

'Hello,' she said, and then looked at Mark with what I thought was disgust and closed her door. Did she know? Could she tell? Did the wrong ones know to choose me? Did my earlier abuse subliminally make me choose 'that one over there'? Or was 'that one' the person I deserved? I was anxious about Mark coming over. I still confuse fear for love. If someone frightens me, I think I might fancy them. I can even take that fear and confuse it further with love.

Mark sat on the bed, and I sat on the desk chair, and then the floor, showing him my record collection. He laughed mockingly at some of the things in my room—my music, my posters, and even my clothes. I remember he thought my tights were 'Nora Batty like.' I wished I had better tights. I thought this was sarcastic banter, like he enjoyed with his friends, so I laughed along. It made me feel part of the gang, but I'd need to toughen up to those insults.

Of course, my Celtic things were hilarious to him. He saw my scarf, my bracelet, my pendant, and my hat.

'What's this thing?' It was a Celtic bucket hat I had had signed and pinned to the wall. He pulled it off and stuck it on his head.

'Who's this on here, then? Roy Aitken?' He collapsed back onto the bed in laughter and screwed up his face. His usual audience of pals was not there, so I laughed too. The hat was a bit silly.

He mocked my posters; one was of some Disney characters.

Embarrassed, I told him I was going to take them down; they were so immature. He raided through more things on my desk. He thought my *Johnny Hates Jazz* tape was crap. I excused it as my sister's, which must have got muddled up. I owned better tapes and some CDs, which I tried to show him.

Mark got me to sit on the bed with him. He touched me on my arms, my legs, and my hands. I felt uncomfortable, but I was too shy to say anything. I jumped up and babbled I don't remember what. My accent was funny to him, and some of the words I used. He tried an Edinburgh accent. He never ran out of things to say. He laughed at his own jokes, and I joined in.

Then he held my hand and we sat together and kissed for a while. I did like it, but I didn't say anything. A boy had kissed me once before, on holiday when I was fifteen, but this was different.

Mark pushed me until I was lying down on the bed and starting kissing and grinding on me. Once again, I didn't say anything. Then he tried to lift my clothing and touch me in places that made me feel extremely awkward.

'Hey, why don't we listen to my records for a bit? I've got The Proclaimers or Talking Heads?' I said as I tried to squirm away.

'What?' He didn't stop.

'I'm a bit nervous, to be honest.'

'Aye, okay.' He didn't stop.

'I've not done this before.' I tried to indicate that I was uncomfortable.

'Uh-huh.' He still didn't stop.

'No,' I said.

He stopped, but then started again. Then he shut the curtains, removed his shirt, and kept kissing me.

'Okay, that's enough. That's about okay,' I said eventually. I felt intimidated, scared, but I still said 'no' multiple times. I put my hand in the way.

Mark looked fed-up. He sat on the bed and sighed. I pulled myself up to sitting, with my back against the headboard. I couldn't get out because the bed was against the wall, so he was in the way. He was staring at the wall.

'Come on,' he said with impatience, pulling me back down to a lying position. He climbed on top of me; then, like the man on holiday, he lifted my skirt and put his hands on me. I wished I'd worn trousers. It was my fault again. I brought him into my bedroom. What did I think would happen?

He kept biting my neck and shoulder. I tried negotiating with him, 'Let's do it tomorrow instead,' but he barked, 'Relax your legs!' I tried holding my knickers up and squirming away, but he succeeded in invading my body.

I knew I was supposed to scream or hit, but I didn't. I gave in. I was paralysed with shock. I stared at the ceiling, concentrating on the cracks, hoping for the pain to end.

Once it was over, Mark lit a cigarette. 'Are you mad at me?' he asked.

I didn't answer.

He laughed. 'You were wet, so you definitely wanted it.'

I wanted to kiss him, but this had gone further than I wanted. My brain froze. I didn't know how to react. I lay still while he cleaned himself up in the side room, which had a sink off it, not a modern ensuite. The communal showers were at the end of the corridor. Once he came back out, I abruptly got up and sat on the edge of the bed.

'You are a weird one,' he said.

I wasn't speaking at all. There were no words. What had happened?

He put his jacket on, and I suddenly didn't want him to leave. I had made him feel awkward. I needed to try to act normal.

'Maybe we can go out sometime. There's this party at the GUU. We could go together or before that?' I suggested, gesturing to a flyer on the wall for the end-of-term bash. He pulled it off and pocketed it.

'Oh yeah, okay.' He gave me a kiss on the cheek, and I walked him all the way to the door. He lit another cigarette and did not look back.

Okay, I thought as I walked all the way back up the stairs. That had not gone well, but he liked me, and I had given him the wrong idea.

I went for a shower and caught myself in the mirror. When I saw the bruises and bite marks, I cried.

TWENTY-EIGHT

" I told myself it was my fault. That it was just what boyfriends and girlfriends do. That I was hung up about sex as I'd experienced something traumatic as a child. Anyhow, I needed to 'do it' sometime. I thought Mark and I could get through it. Next time, I'd forget my frigid nonsense and it would be okay.

When I called Mark the next day, whispering on the communal phone, Diane was behind me, listening in, tapping her feet, telling me to hurry up. When I mentioned the bruises and bite marks, Mark mocked me and said I must have sensitive skin. When I told him that I was not ready, he said I misled him, and I should be careful not to give men 'signs' but that we had 'fun'.

I asked him if we could go for a walk in the Botanic Gardens. He said he was finishing off his Masters and would see me at the party at the end of term. He said he was busy, and I needed to understand that.

I survived not hearing from Mark for two weeks.

That should have been my first magical time with my first, my boyfriend.

After the rape, there were phases where I was fine, but I surrendered to hollowness when I closed the door of my room, surveyed the scene of the crime. I cried a lot. I felt anxiety like I hadn't before.

I recognised the feelings I had endured as a child, although I hadn't processed them at that younger age. Walking up the stairs in the halls was overwhelming; I had to relive it every day. I would look over my shoulder, feeling that he was there.

I started to see all men as threats until they proved otherwise. I was careful not to give signs. I acted overly confident to cover up all these feelings. I didn't want anyone to know my secret.

TWENTY-NINE

MY COURSE WAS A RELIEF, as I excelled academically, but one girl took a dislike to my faked brashness. She couldn't deal with my self-assured performance when I was such a scruff. She was popular, so perhaps she took exception to me existing, to me grabbing some of her attention in class. Tina was the female Mark—the top dog in the gang who sat behind me in lectures.

I remember how she was with her boyfriend, Cameron, a sweet boy with a good sense of humour. He had acne and bad dress sense and wore braces and glasses. He was not pretty. She was beautiful, with smooth, peachy skin. Her jet-black hair combined with bright blue eyes and high cheekbones made even women stare. She would put Cameron down, and he would still follow her around as she eyed up the other boys and flirted right in front of him.

It was obvious she had come to university for a man. She made an excellent decision in finally dating him, although everyone was surprised. She tidied him up. He was her little puppy, and puppies grow into loyal dogs; no matter how many times you kick them, they love you more. She'd get bored with him sexually, but she would gain a loyal, decent man who wouldn't bore her and would never cheat. He wouldn't dare.

Malcolm, one of her cronies, had written a scathing description of me in the magazine. It was all fun in his eyes. Everyone on our course got a roasting, apart from Tina's tribe, members of which were all praised for their style, looks, and personalities. Basically, I was fat and ugly, according to his article about the girls he rated from 1 to 100. I had shoved him when he'd skipped the refectory queue in front of me, making him drop his food. Tina was offended by my reaction. I thought he got off lightly.

I was sitting at the squares' table with the Goth, the geek, and the Asian girl. Tina had recently reported the latter to the Dean for being smelly. She sashayed over from the cool table, where they had obviously been discussing my behaviour.

'You need to apologise to Malcolm.' Tina was going to deal with it.

She had some nerve. I laughed in her face, partly in shock. This took her by surprise. She wasn't used to being laughed at.

'Unbelievable,' she muttered as she walked away, shaking her head. She wanted to tell me off, but I wasn't taking it. She didn't know my newly found bite was because I was scared about my recent secret.

We had been warned to secure our lockers. Some money was stolen every year. I never locked mine. I was scatty and late to lectures, always rushing. Halfway through the lecture, while I was getting my notebook out, I realised I had left my purse in my locker. I rushed back before the next class.

My last twenty-pound note, which was to last the week, was gone.

I hurried back into the lecture theatre to tell the lecturer. He rolled his eyes and basically said that he had told me so. I asked him to remind everyone not to make the same mistake as me. As he reluctantly did so, I heard giggling behind me. Tina waved a twenty-pound note at me as her friends, including Malcolm, tittered.

Cameron looked embarrassed but joined in the laughter. He had to back her.

'Tina, what are you like?' I had made another enemy.

I take my anger out on all the wrong people all the time, but Tina deserved the attitude, and so did Malcolm. I was a coiled spring ready to snap at any time.

THE TERM ROLLED ON, and it was time for the hall's bash at the union nightclub, imaginatively called 'The Club'. I hadn't heard anything from Mark, but I hoped he might attend with the gang. It was my last chance to salvage something from this mess and forget it had happened the way it did.

He could be my boyfriend, and that silly misunderstanding would fade into the past. I'd relax more next time. It was my first time. Losing my virginity was painful, and I was nervous. He'd understand. We could be together.

I arrived late to the party as the pub crawl with Dawn and James and the two Alasdairs went on longer than planned. I didn't want to tell them why I was in a hurry to get to the GUU.

Mark and the boys were there. But he didn't speak to me. He just nodded a 'hello' when I approached. I spoke to Joe, who was the oldest and sweetest, as I did not want to crowd Mark. The other boys ignored me, apart from David, who made fun of my outfit. They all seemed bored with me. I tried not to care, as I sat with them, but as Joe was speaking to me, I glanced up to see Mark wasn't there. I turned around, and he was dancing with Elizabeth. She was in fourth year, studying Biology. Although a well-liked girl in our halls, she was quite old-fashioned in her dress and demeanour. Even her haircut was boring. I turned back, my face burning with jealousy.

I danced with a group of girls for a while, and when I came back from the toilets, Mark and the gang were gone. To my relief, Elizabeth was still there.

Everyone packed up the following week to go home for the summer holidays. I couldn't find Mark. I called and there was no answer. I walked past his flat, and it looked like no one was there. Perhaps they moved out earlier than planned. I went to his lab. His photo was on the wall. He was never there.

I blamed myself. Why wasn't I normal? No wonder he didn't like me. I was frigid or something. I must have imagined the Elizabeth thing. He couldn't surely go out with the girl who lived five doors down the corridor from me. Back at halls, I paused outside her door but stopped myself from knocking to ask.

WHEN I RETURNED to Glasgow after the summer holidays, I still half-hoped Mark and I could get together. I believed I'd see him again. This time, I was older. This time, things would work out. I walked alone to all the places we had been, and then on to the beer bar, where I saw the back of a familiar head. It was Joe, playing on the fruit machine.

'Hiya,' he said. He looked pleased to see me. I'd lost a lot of weight. I was thinner, more worthy of being a girlfriend. Joe was always the kindest of them. He showed me a picture of his current girlfriend, Belinda. She looked old to me. I was nineteen, and Joe was thirty-two.

'How's Mark doing? Not seen him, but I suppose he'll be finished his masters, of course.'

Joe paused his playing and turned to me. 'Mark?' he raised his eyebrows.

For a second, I thought something terrible had happened to him. It had been over three months; anything could have occurred in that time.

'Mark's engaged. Totally loved up,' he said, looking right at me for the flicker of a reaction. He got none.

'Lassie called Elizabeth. They are getting married in May.'

It can't be her—the Elizabeth I knew! Maybe he had a girlfriend all the time and never mentioned it.

I changed the subject. I wanted to know more, but I didn't want Mark to know I wanted to know more. What was the point? He was getting married, and that was that. I couldn't get him back. I never ever properly had him. *Did he force her? She was a well-known virgin. Was she less frigid?* I said none of these things. I acted cool.

'Married? Ha! That's for mugs,' I joked, acting like I did not care one bit.

Joe laughed and nodded. He was thirty-two, unmarried, and still hanging around the university with teenagers. I knew that would go down well with him.

It was getting out of hand—how easily I could pretend the opposite of how I truly felt. I spoke on and on about how well I was doing, how amazing my course was, how I was top of the class, how much money I was going to make.

'If you are going to make all that money, maybe I should marry you,' Joe said.

It was a joke, but I considered Joe for a while. Perhaps just to get back at Mark or even to see him again. I hoped that everything I said would be relayed back to Mark to show I didn't care.

I never asked if it was *my* Elizabeth. She had left in June, qualified from her course. I didn't know whether she was following up her degree with a PhD or whether she had found a job. Today, I'd be stalking the whole lot of them on social media. In those days, you never saw people ever again unless you had their address or phone number. Even then, you would have to call and hope they were in.

I walked back to the halls. It had been four months since the 'event' between Mark and me. Since then, he had met someone else, fallen in love, established a relationship and got engaged—all in that short time. Maybe it wasn't her. Maybe he'd had a long-term girlfriend he was cheating on.

THIRTY

Fun fact of the day: I have considered throwing Mark in front of a train, but CCTV footage and mobile phones would make that difficult these days. Also, I don't know his daily movements, so how would I know when to do the deed? I have shelved that idea.

But it was true—he married Elizabeth! If it weren't for me, they never would have met. I invited him to that party.

I saw them years later in the Clockwork Orange, Glasgow's famous subway. I was soaked to the skin. (Never forget an umbrella in Glasgow!) They hopped on together at Kelvinbridge.

I don't think they recognised me—it had been years, after all, and I doubted that I figured in their fairy tale. I was staring right at them. They looked over, and then they bowed their heads and started laughing. Did they notice me and remember? Did she know? What were they laughing at? Rape?

They call it rape now. But back then, I thought it

wasn't, as I invited him in, I gave in. I told him to stop, and then I just let it happen. Then he wanted Elizabeth.

I remember how I had felt sick and another feeling—not jealousy, but humiliation. I remember how powerless I was, my face reddening as wee, cute Elizabeth and handsome Mark, her rapist husband, carried on giggling on the subway.

She was worth affection and love. I was worth discarding after use. I was nothing.

Second Section—University

- Mark
- Elizabeth
- Tina

Glasgow, party, book, extras

THIRTY-ONE

'HIYA! Oh, where you off to today?' Preston says as he comes in unannounced. I must lock my door, but he has a key for emergencies, so he'd get in anyway. He has seen my rucksack, my sparkly notebook, my keys, and the train tickets all lying on the table.

'Glasgow,' I reply curtly. I have no reason to lie. People go to Glasgow all the time, and that is where I am going. It is written on the tickets, so he might have seen that already and then he would know if I lied.

He pauses with arched eyebrows, pouts, and waits for an explanation.

'For your information, and so you can keep your files up to date, I will let you know I am going through to Glasgow to register as an extra in a movie,' I explain, stuffing the sparkly notebook into the rucksack.

'An extra in a movie? Oooh, okay. What movie?' He sits, ready to be served tea. He must have seen the time on the tickets and knows I don't need to leave right away.

'I saw an announcement on Facebook.' I look it up on my phone and show him the poster that states, 'Extras wanted—all ages, shapes and sizes for a Scottish period drama. No experience required.' It's on the bucket list. I think I am beyond getting the lead role.

'Oh, wow ... I'm getting diggy view everywhere.'

'Diggy view?' I question.

'When you get a feeling about something that happened before.'

'*Déjà vu.*' I pronounce it correctly.

'All right D.J. Voo, then,' Preston says, emphasising every syllable. 'My pal Justine and I were extras in *Mary Queen of Scots.*' He gets to his story of the day. 'She was a wench, and I was just ... What was I?' He clicks his fingers as he mentally reaches for the right description of his character. 'I was some random peasant. Basically, everyone was wearing rags unless you were a main character. We were there the whole day. I could hardly stop looking at the camera. I couldn't help it. You know when they tell you not to do something and you have to do it; like when you see a sign saying, "Don't Press This Button!"— that was me.' He laughs. 'Then they gave *her* a bloody line.' He laughs again and then pauses. 'She must have said it every possible way a person can say six words. I said, "Fuck's sake, Justine, you're no Jodie Foster." In the end, I was in it for about three seconds in a crowd scene.'

'And Justine?'

'They cut her out.' I laugh at this, and he continues. 'Anyway... all the way to Glasgow just for that, though?'

'They want to measure heights and take a photo,' I explain.

'Is there not an Edinburgh one?' he asks. I explain I missed that date.

'Can you not send in a photo? Honestly. There is such a thing as email,' whines Preston. He is clearly at a loose end today; he wants company.

'A friend of mine is having a book launch in Byres Road, so I am going to that as well. And I might go to the museum or the university for a look about.' I am getting too close to telling all. I don't mention the party I plan to attend.

'Friend?' He curls his lips as he asks.

Here is something you find out when you're terminally ill: There's a stark difference between a friend and an acquaintance. Preston is my friend. This person in Glasgow is neither, just another human—and barely that.

'On your own?' He raises one eyebrow this time. He is angling for an invite.

'I'm meeting someone too,' I say, so I can go alone.

'Who?'

'A guy off Tinder.'

'Shut up! Ha!' He laughs and claps his hands with delight. 'Fuck off, then!' he says as a goodbye. Preston knows a lie when he hears one, and a brush off, but he accepts that as the punchline to the conversation.

I HEAD to Glasgow on the train for the extras sign up. Miss Moleman's obituary is in the newspaper I picked up on the way to the station. It's three weeks since she passed away. The local paper is always outrageously late with death notices. 'The well-loved primary schoolteacher died in her sleep of natural causes.'

'Well-loved,' I snort, and the man opposite looks up. I smile at him and cough as if something was caught in my throat.

Unsurprisingly, the announcement of her death on social media did not reflect that sentiment. A few wrote the usual platitude nonsense under the article, but there were random uncomplimentary comments too: 'Auld witch' and 'At last—only the good die young'. Disrespectful, frowned the Facebook mob. I tapped a quick 'Thoughts and prayers'. My finger hovered over the 'Like' button on the article, but people might notice that. The articles didn't mention the ruler, which was strange, in a way, but pleasing that no one thought it significant. I knew it was there, and that's the main thing.

I couldn't find my Glasgow targets on Facebook for a long time. They aren't my usual sites, but I couldn't find them on Twitter or

LinkedIn either. Why are the people I look for so secretive? Are they spies or in the witness-protection programme?

Mark's name is common, so there were hundreds of them. Her name was tricky. How to spell Elizabeth? Obvious, you would think, but she could be Beth, Liz, Lizzie, Lizzy, even Lilibet. I eventually found him through his daughter—a Betty, named after her mother.

Betty was not shy. She had an open Facebook page with over a thousand friends. She studied Pharmacology at university, like her dad. I added her as a friend, as we share two mutual friends who are band people in Glasgow. Scotland is small sometimes. It took me a while to be sure she was the right girl, but I soon saw tagged photos of Mark and followed them to his less-obvious profile.

His was a closed page, but a couple of posts were open to view. One of the pictures was of him and his daughter on her eighteenth birthday. Mark's arm was around her, and their heads were leaning together. He was smiling proudly, while she seemed excited. His daughter looked the same age that I was when he raped me.

He looked like a devoted father. He was a chain smoker, so he should look ravaged. Instead, he looked rugged; the bastard was still attractive. He was dressed similarly in all the photos. I wondered if he was wearing the same jacket he had all those years ago. He had no reason to change his signature style. I guess, in coming up for thirty years, it must be a new version of the same style: Jacket Mark Five.

On his page, the other things he shared publicly were creepy, sexist memes. Jokes about women being useful for making sandwiches. Posts mocking women who look ugly the morning after without makeup. Posts showing curvaceous young women bending over and leery men ogling their knickers or their boobs. He has liked pages called 'Hot Chicks' and 'Sexy Babes'. Underneath another photo of his daughter, he has commented, 'Beautiful'. It's like two different people! Craig has added underneath, 'You and Liz'—*Liz! She is a Liz!*—'are going to have problems with your gorgeous daughter.'

Well, let's hope she doesn't come across any men like Mark.

THE BUCKET LIST   117

I kept looking and shuddered at a comment he made on a date-rape case. He thought it unfair on the boy being accused. He made a comment about how women ruin men's lives by making stuff up. What was she doing drunk and dressed up like that anyway? My blood ran cold. I wasn't drunk. I had been wearing an ankle-length skirt. He liked the short-skirted girls in the photos, but as he commented later on the rape case, 'Boys will be boys!'

All young Betty talks about on Facebook is her upcoming wedding in Glasgow and how Mum and Dad's anniversary is the same day. She's clearly so happy to be getting married at Glasgow University, where Mum and Dad got married. *How the hell did I miss that fantastic event?* I must have been in the same postcode when it happened, and I wasn't even invited. Then she talked about her reception party, which was to be held at the university union. 'Thanks to my lovely Daddy for paying for it all.'

Lovely Daddy! I made a note of the date.

I think back to the party at the end of term in the GUU venue, the rape, and how I felt after it. I close my eyes on the train, picturing it all.

THIRTY-TWO

"*Why hadn't I gone home with my hall pals that night and never met that gang of boys? Boys? No ... MEN. They were in their late twenties and early thirties back then, and I was eighteen. I still blame myself. I still hate myself for inviting him over.*

My life of pretending started in earnest then. I'd done it as a child, but this was when I honed my skills.

I felt like an abomination. I felt powerless. I started lying to people, saying I was fine, putting up a happy, fake persona when I just wanted someone to understand. Someone to hug me and tell me that everything would be fine. To this day, my ability to fake normality is incredible.

He possessed all the power before, during, and after. I was confused because I genuinely liked Mark, and I wondered what I had done wrong. I felt angry with him. Angry with myself for being gullible enough to trust him, for not shouting, 'How dare you!' I felt ashamed. I felt it was my fault. Then I wondered how ...

I never suggested any of it. I wasn't drunk, never wore or said anything to encourage him—not that that was important. I felt guilty.

Maybe he was right. Maybe I did want it. Maybe I needed persuading. No, just because I wanted to kiss him didn't give him the license to grope, and the rest! I said 'No.' I said, 'Stop!' and 'Enough!' several times. Rape is not always about being jumped in an alley like in a television drama. They never show what it is like to be raped by someone you know, someone you like or love.

I felt weak for not reporting him back then, but would reporting it have been worth the headache? I couldn't report it. They wouldn't believe me. He was the gang leader of the coolest guys and a PhD student.

Around that time, a girl was raped in Kelvin Way, minutes from us and remarkably close to the boys' place. We had walked it that first night to get to their flat. My fellow students, watching the report with me on the communal TV, said things like, 'What the hell was she doing walking down there at night?' or 'It's so dark there. She never should have been on her own' or 'What did she expect? Probably drunk.' This was a girl simply walking home from the train, who was dragged into the park and raped under a bush. What would they say about me, who invited him in and upstairs to sit on my bed?

All my life, I've had to try hard not to fear all men, to overcome betrayal by someone I liked. I felt like a slut. I felt like a victim.

I ARRIVE in Argyle Street for the movie extras sign-up before I'm due. There is an updated announcement on Facebook that they have enough females and need big men, preferably with beards. I walk along opposite the Kelvingrove Museum, thinking maybe I can still put my name down. The queue is huge. I have never seen so many heavyset, bearded men in my life. There are at least a hundred of them, and the queue is static. I give up, as it's raining; I forgot my rule of bringing an umbrella, and, bizarrely, my PVC jacket is getting wet through.

I turn around and walk along Kelvin Way, skirt the Union Building and head up University Avenue to Byres Road. I march along with my earphones in. It's a classic iPod—old-fashioned now; I carried my Sony Walkman about when I strode up and down this road as a student. I listen to the same songs from the '90s I saved on the iPod.

I go into a café. I couldn't afford a café when I was a student, although they are full of students now. Student loans had just started when I was there, and the thought of debt scared me. Others in Tina's gang were living it up, buying cars, getting haircuts at Taylor Ferguson's and buying cool clothes. I was running around in a banger, wearing clothes from jumble sales, like I was stuck in the eighties.

I love the brightness of the day, despite the rain. *Is this my last spring?* I probably have two more. I am near the Hillhead Library. I am surprised it is still there after all these years. I was going to go after the film casting, so now I'm the first here. My primary purpose is to get some information, but the book launch is handy. Tina will be here later. The book she has written is a self-help book: *Help yourself.*

Holy shit, the self-centred cow is still lecturing others how to live their lives. She helped herself to the contents of my purse, all right, I think, laughing out loud. A woman looks over at me as I'm walking up the Byres Road, laughing to myself. I cough again.

ONCE IN THE LIBRARY, I find a book on foraging. I forage through the foraging book for miracle health cures, because, yes, cancer patients also tend to research natural remedies and hippy advice. We're made to feel guilty about our disease. We get suggestions to figure out what we did wrong with our nutrition and lifestyle. I can handle it, but what about my Callum? Will he pick up that if Mum had drunk more kombucha or made a bit more effort to meditate, she'd still be alive?

It also tells me poisonous things to avoid. It is innocuous to look up a book in a library. You don't start Googling 'poison' on the Internet: it's a fount of information but all traceable. I make photocopies of the relevant chapters and note the book title. I might buy it later.

I learn from the book that a fair bit of the natural world can do you in. Lots of poisonous things are lying around. This is handy, as I can't go to a chemist to purchase deadly items. They would ask a lot of questions and, again, it's traceable. I tuck the photocopied papers into the back of the sparkly notebook.

Tina is here now, setting up. Her books are stacked high on a trestle table. The subheading is: *Forgive Yourself, Live Happy.*

I bet you did, love. I consider letting off the fire alarm during the launch, to piss her off. I don't want to kill her for petty theft and being a bossy bitch. That's not enough reason.

Cameron is here, smiling at everyone and looking proud. I've never seen Tina smile; she has never had to make that effort.

Cameron is slim and fit, older as we all are, but looking well. He looks better as an older man. It is obvious from their Facebook pages that he still dotes on her. She is free to be the bitch as much as she ever was. Her beauty still astounds him.

Most of us, when young, go for the good-looking guy like Mark. They don't put their ladies on a pedestal like Cameron does. He has stayed sweet, funny, kind, and passable looking.

Tina did well, and Cameron treats her like a princess. Nothing has changed, apart from that she looks disappointed with ageing, and he looks better and happier than her. *What a shame. Poor Tina.*

She has already signed a pile of books. I go over and I am pleasant to her, although she is standoffish. I didn't bloody like her years ago, and I don't like her now, but I make sure I am seen at the beginning. I take a quick snap of her face on the six-foot-tall banner with her giant signature. I sit at the back and note that it's busier than I expected, but no wonder, there is free entry with tea and coffee.

I'm not sure she remembers me. I saw a flicker of recognition, but I'll make sure to tag her later on Facebook so she doesn't forget I was here. She won't notice me among all the fat, desperate women; I look like them, so she won't miss me either.

I wonder how long these things take and whether I'll have time to come back for the signing. I don't want to come back, but I want it to look as if I was there the whole time.

I could buy her book from Amazon later and fake the signature. I should stop giving my business to Amazon. It's against my principles, but it's a habit. Sports Direct is also on the bad list and Primark—how many 50p knickers are necessary? I decide I'll have to Amazon the book and not come back for one, as I haven't the time.

I change my mind as I pass the pile of pre-signed books on my way out. I nick one right into my bag—*problem solved*. It's not difficult to steal. No one expects petty crime in the library. It's not the done thing at these events in the West End. I glimpse the price on the back: £19.99. *That much?* She owes me twenty quid anyway. I'll let her off with the penny.

I head to the university, back along University Avenue. I'm seconds away from the union building when I almost walk into him. It's Mark. He is here. He should be at the GUU for the post-wedding reception or meal.

I panic, stop, face the wall, and hold my breath. Before I know it, he walks right by me. I follow him as he crosses to the university main buildings.

He liked it here, met girls here, met me here before he met Elizabeth—the one he loved. We are in the quads. *Where is he going? Some office?* The wedding took place in the memorial chapel. The photos were taken here in the quads earlier, someone must have left something behind, and he has been sent to get it. I give up, leave him there and turn and go to the GUU. I wasn't expecting that meeting, and I can't deal with him yet. He never left the city, never even left this area. *Have these people no imagination?*

I head up the steps to the door and go in, nod to the doorman, and say, 'The wedding.' He glances up and nods back. I look up. It's an impressive venue, mind you. I walk up the wide stone steps to the first landing. The debating chamber on the right is where the wedding reception is. I saw a band here once at one 'Daft Friday' event, but I can't remember who they were. I don't think it was Goodbye Mr. Mackenzie. The nightclub is gone as such; they knocked down the previous extension several years ago and built a fancier one.

I went back to the Queen Margaret Union after first year. I went through my second gothic phase. GUU had too many rugby boys and beer-drinking competitions. Memories of Mark haunted me there.

My back hurts again. I hope my cancer hasn't spread. I've been walking a long distance today, so that might be the cause.

I am dressed in black leggings that could pass for tights, a short black skirt and a white top, a PVC jacket (now melted in the rain), and I'm carrying a rucksack.

In the toilets, I change into a pinny I brought and dump the ruined jacket. Bloody Glasgow rain is like acid. I am dressed like the servers at the wedding, in a black and white uniform, but also like a cleaner, so they don't question me as being part of the waitstaff. No one notices women over forty-five anyway, especially if they are overweight service staff. They aren't viable breeding humans anymore, just the cleaner, the waitress, or the shop assistant. No one would notice Tracey, for example.

There is no point being a glamorous murderer or spy. Every man and woman would turn and stare at you. A solid, obese potato-face and no one can even describe you. 'Face like a tattie?' or 'Round face and average hair?' People like that are very difficult to describe. They wouldn't find you in a million years. I am like everyone's mum or granny, and no one gives me a second look.

The meal is being served. Mark had been sent to pick up a jacket left behind once the speeches were all done, and he passes me on the landing again before he heads into the room. I peek in and see that Elizabeth is quite changed. She's chubby now but has the same boring haircut. Old Liz is still old-fashioned. I spot Mark again, paying no attention to the wife but chatting up the young waitress. I go downstairs to the basement and beer bar, avoiding the staff and guests.

Finding a cleaner's cupboard, I take out a mop. I go back up, hovering about that landing outside the reception room and the rooms off it. Mark comes out after the meal. I expect him to go to the toilets, but instead, he turns to go up the stairs. I follow him up but on the staircase on the other side. Maybe there is something else up here for him to fetch. A surprise for the happy couple?

The stairs are wide and stone, and they are just a little too shallow; you feel you are taking a lot of steps to get anywhere. I go up the right-hand steps and to the next halfway level with the huge stained-glass window. While I am on the halfway level, he turns and looks back from the main staircase again.

Does he recognise me? I hear love-song music in my head. He half-smiles. My heart jumps. Maybe he regrets it all. Maybe he wonders where I have been all those years. He couldn't face me after that night, so he settled for her. He has been looking for me for years, but he is stuck with you-know-who …

Then it's clear he has no idea who I am, as he turns away and carries on with his errand.

He doesn't stop at the second-floor level but turns to the left again and up further to a floor I have never been on. I don't know what's up there—rooms, I assume. I never went up there as a student, and I'm not going now. He wanders around like he owns the place. I stay on the second-floor landing.

I wait at the back wall of the large landing for him to come back down. What goes up must come down. He is gone for some time before he appears again, heading back down to my level. He is still handsome—Harrison Ford, but Glaswegian. Now I reassess, I think I exaggerated that memory, but I can still see where I was coming from. He hasn't changed at all.

THIRTY-THREE

" Whenever I suffered a bad experience, I changed everything. After the rape and the subsequent ghosting, I went home that summer and came back two stone lighter with a crop hairstyle. It didn't suit my face, but I didn't want to look too attractive and encourage more unwanted attention.

Other times of heartache, I've moved furniture, repainted rooms, and moved cities. But the classic was always the hair change. I've sported all colours and styles: several mullets, short and spiky, glossy bobs. I've been Jessica Rabbit and Liza Minnelli. I had to change like a chameleon.

Mark never had to change. Everything was the way he wanted. He never moved away or changed his dress. It was always just right for him.

When I stepped forward to meet him at the bottom of the steps. I saw him look right at me. I heard music in my head again, and I felt the urge to kiss him.

There was no one up there. It was dark and deserted.

Brian throbbed in my head, telling me I could change things this time—make it right for ME. Then it all flashed before me. It all built up in me until I relived it all again.

'What are you doing?' he asked, and then his final words, 'Who are you?'

'No one,' I said.

I stepped back, as if to let him pass, then I turned and spun and hit him hard in the chest with the mop, making him stagger back against the wall. A hard couple of bashes with the handle knocked him to the floor, unconscious. I gave him a quick, solid kick to the head. I heard a crack, and he was dead. I am quite strong, but I even surprised myself.

I pulled Mark up and rolled him down the main staircase. He landed on the halfway landing with the beautiful backdrop of the stained-glass window. I stared at it for a few seconds; it's wasn't very colourful, apart from some blue squares of glass. The crest of arms of Glasgow University, where Mark spent most of his days, looked over his crumpled body. I studied the symbols of St Mungo: the tree and the bird, the bell, the salmon with the ring in its mouth, the mace, and the book of learning. I tried to find something of significance, but I found nothing. Then I moved on down the steps, avoiding his body, and onto the first floor again, where the party was still going.

The connection from the main building to the extension was quite similar to how it was before, when I was at university. I found the door that led me to a corridor, and then travelled right, along to the extension. I assumed everyone would have run out by then to see the carnage on the stair. I could probably even have returned to the scene in my server disguise. That's how *murderers behave, don't they? But this was not a murder; it was an execution.*

I didn't go back. I walked along the corridor as far as it went. The end part had all changed. There was a modern nightclub instead of The Club where the hall's party took place all those years ago. After wiping the mop down, I left it in the toilets and removed my pinny. I found a fire exit, which are always well-marked. It led onto a lane at the back of the building so I wasn't seen. I headed up the hill and down Great George Street, back into Byres Road.

Adrenaline fired me on. I walked past Hillhead Underground, the subway. Its warmth and smell hit me. Fun fact of the day: I once read its smell came from Archangel tar that was used to grease the cables, mixed with dust and oil. It wafted up the escalators like a warm air, wrapped me so thickly I felt like I could taste it, bite it.

I WALK past the library to check if Tina's book launch is finished. She is still there. I think of popping in again but decide against it. I'll make out I was there the whole time and she never noticed. She wouldn't be looking for me afterwards for a chat.

I remember to post on social media that I got the book and include a close-up photograph of the signature inside.

I imagine the conversation with police or detectives.

'Did you see this woman?' the cop would ask.

'Yes,' Tina would say.

'Was she here the whole time, at your book launch?'

'I don't know. I think so.'

'She has your book. She tagged you on Facebook,' Cameron would helpfully interject.

'Well, she must have been there. Yes, I think I saw her at the back.'

Sure, Tina, I was there the whole time. You simply forgot.

Heading home on the train from Queen Street, I smile to myself, looking out the window. I don't care if the other passengers stare at me. I was cold after losing my jacket, so I bought a tracksuit and a ridiculous hat at the Celtic shop. I wear them with a smile all the way home on the train.

Second Section—University

- ~~Mark~~
- ~~Elizabeth~~
- ~~Tina~~

Glasgow, party, book, extras

Third Section—Island

- Eric
- Brenda
- Simone
- Steve

THIRTY-FOUR

 'Why can't you find one who isn't a Walter Mitty?'
Mum used to say to me.

Eric seemed harmless enough. But the whole thing
was faked. Or was it a game, an elaborate game? Either
way, he was in a made-up world of his own.

It lasted years. Four years from beginning to end. I'd
been on the island three years by the time I met him. My
marriage had failed a short time after Callum was born.
I'd been concentrating on being a single mother, but I
used to sing at the weekends, when Callum's dad
took him.

I was singing when I first saw him looking up at me.
He was with his girlfriend, who watched me too, but also
glanced nervously at him, as his stare was so intense in
my direction.

He was handsome—tall and slim with dark hair and
deep-set eyes. I thought he could almost model if he
stood up straighter. His squat, plain girlfriend had dirty-

blonde hair stuck flatly to her head. Her wide-set eyes made it look like she had a squint.

There was nothing behind her eyes. Preston would call them 'nothing eyes', 'dead eyes' or 'blank eyes'. No fun, personality, or humour. You knew she would never laugh at your jokes.

They made an odd couple to look at. She was as overweight as I am now. Also, her teeth had a gap at the bottom, right in the middle. My eyes were drawn to the blackness.

'THIS IS ERIC. He's a bit weird, but a cracking drummer.' My friend William gestured to the handsome man he had brought to watch me sing in a concert, as he was considering us all getting together to form a band. William was the potential guitarist. Eric, Mr. Model, never spoke, but I was aware of him watching my every move. Mr. Model kept staring, and then he let out a weird laugh that made him seem strange and made William roll his eyes.

'Now, William, don't speak about Eric like that,' said the girlfriend, whose name was Brenda. Her tone was motherly and well-spoken, verging on patronising.

The band got together, and we had some rehearsals. William dropped out, so we found another guitarist, and Eric brought a couple of friends to play accordion and fiddle. I got my male company that way.

Eric was musical and a bit silly, once he opened up. I grew fond of him over the years. We had a joint interest, and he seemed to like me—perhaps a bit too much, which he didn't hide from anyone, including his girlfriend. He told me he and Brenda had been together ten years, since they were teenagers. He was twenty-eight by the time I met him, and I was thirty-two.

He'd say inappropriate things sometimes; not rude, just random.

It was as if he wasn't listening to the conversation that was going on but had to get out whatever popped into his head. I started to make excuses for him, like Brenda and William did. I became protective of him.

People noticed him following me around. My friend Lol (her mother had named her Lola, but she hated it) and I were singing at a wedding in the local church. When we came out, we took photos of the bride's carriage driving away. She sent me a photo she had taken of the carriage and the happy couple with Eric in the background leaning against a wall, watching it all. I didn't even know he was there. She thought it hilarious.

'Your wee lurking pet was there,' Lol laughed. She called him Lurkio from then on. I mentioned my singing at the wedding to the boys at band practice. Eric said he liked my dress and described it in perfect detail.

'You should wear that dress to band.' Eric didn't hide that he was following me around. He said it in front of all the band members. They just looked at me and shook their heads with embarrassment.

I started dating a chap I met through Susan, who was fine enough. Steve was gregarious company, quite witty, and we would go out to dinner sometimes. He wasn't that nice to me. I didn't care because I did not care about him much either. He never treated me well from the beginning, so I never got the chance to grow fond of him.

Steve took me to dinner one time on the west side of the island. The reason for the trip was that the restaurant's owner had recently been widowed, and he wanted an excuse to meet her. She had been left the restaurant and all the land. Steve said she was a super prospect. I'd grown used to accompanying him to meet my replacement. At one dinner party we attended, he went as far as to tell the table he thought women were 'mere chattels'. I pretended not to know what that meant, while all the women at the table gasped; I knew he'd done it for attention. When I think of it now, I wish I had left at that.

Another time, I mentioned that William had started seeing a woman in town.

'Why didn't you tell me there was a single woman on the island I hadn't met before?' he stormed. 'I wish I had known. I'd have liked to meet her.'

He was always looking for an upgrade. I didn't love him. I wasn't in deep enough to get anything more than ticked off. I complained about his treatment, and he walked out. I didn't care; I let him go. But still, I was alone, bringing up a child, and it seemed disappointing. I wondered what was wrong with me. I still wanted my prince. Even boring Brenda got her handsome man. I was jealous of her for that, at least.

Eric started popping around when it wasn't band rehearsal time. Initially, he devised excuses of having forgotten something. Random drumsticks were left or cases. Then it was to give me something, anything he had seen in the music shop, a shaker, a mike cover. After a month or so, he would pop in for no reason other than that he fancied a cup of tea.

He told me, in between music chat, that he wasn't happy. He hated his job, his life, and even Brenda. He said he would hide in his shed to get away from her. When I think about the hours I listened, I should have considered a career in counselling. Lol noticed, as sometimes she would be leaving just as he arrived, or she'd arrive and he'd be there.

'You know he is in love with you?' she'd say, raising her eyebrows. 'That or obsessed.'

Susan had noticed him hanging around too. 'He obviously likes you. You have a lot in common with music ...' she probed.

'So what! He is with Brenda, and that's that'! I'd answer, changing the subject. By then, they were engaged. He didn't remember proposing. Brenda said it was time they got married, and his mum and brother insisted it needed to happen. He said he had no choice.

Having Eric's attention made me feel special. Brenda was plain.

In contrast, and partly due to having an admirer, I became more flamboyant.

'I need you in my life,' Eric insisted one night. 'You make this whole situation bearable. '

Something changed with him saying that. I was thrilled with being wanted. I sometimes wonder if I ever love anyone, or maybe I am in love with being loved. He kept hanging around, and I was happy to see him.

Late one night, when I was sure Brenda would be checking the clock as to why he wasn't home, he opened up and told me his abuse story.

He was out one night underage drinking as a seventeen-year-old. He was drugged and woke up between the couple who owned the pub. I was shocked and saddened at how common this was: people damaged by abuse for years after the event.

He said he had been normal until then. After that, he was ill with fear and mistrust. I recognised that feeling. That was when he met Brenda, and she looked after him. He trusted her, and he told her his secret. He said she'd tell his story if he left her.

I was astonished at her emotional blackmail, but it made some sense of his inability to leave. That meek, blank-eyed, polite, dumpy girl was totally in control.

'It wish it had ended years ago, but she wanted us to move in together, and I felt I needed to. My mum and brother think I'm weird, so I won't get anyone else. And she and I work together well; she's sensible, stable,' Eric said, as a note in her favour. 'And now she wants to marry, so that's where I am. I can't get out. I can't leave.'

My heart broke for him.

Then, randomly, he added, 'Would you ever have an affair?'

'No. Anyway, I am single,' I answered nervously. 'I don't have a husband to cheat on.' I thought I was being smart and hoped he'd change tack. I was also offended by the suggestion.

'I mean with someone who is taken already,' he said boldly. For one of the only times in his life, he looked me straight in the eye.

'No!' I answered, knowing he was referring to himself. I didn't fill in the empty silence, which made him go on. 'So ... would you ...? If I wasn't with her, would you go out with me?' I should have told him to get out, but I was lonely, and I felt challenged by the cheek of the question.

Stupidly, I answered, 'I don't know. Yes. Hypothetically, if you weren't with Brenda I would. You are a good-looking boy, and we get on. Why wouldn't I?' I sealed my fate then.

I would never have an affair with someone who was taken. The women around here would call me for everything. It was a small island in many ways, so everyone would know, and gossip loved this place. I should have said a simple, 'No.' That would have prevented what happened next.

THIRTY-FIVE

STEVE, whom I hadn't heard from in months, suddenly decided he couldn't live without me, despite eyeing up every available woman on the island. I told him it was no use. I didn't want to waste his time like he did mine. If I had not had my head turned and been preoccupied with Eric, I might have considered being his doormat again, but I had plenty going on.

Steve kept on pestering me, showering me with gifts and flowers. Suddenly, two men wanted me at once. It was flattering ... and wearing.

I tried to be friends with Steve and tell him about Eric and his stresses, how he was offloading on me. I was out walking with Steve one day when Eric sent me a text message. He and Brenda were away in Gretna. The text read:

I've done it now—got married. Also bought a set of maracas.

It was totally unexpected. Was this planned? Did she surprise him? You can't just run off to Gretna these days and marry; the paperwork needs to be arranged beforehand.

Steve asked me why he was texting. I told him Eric was always texting, so much so that Lol called him Sir Text-a-Lot, but this text was something else. I told him the happy news.

'Why is he texting you that?' he huffed.

'I told you. He tells me everything. Did you not hear anything I was saying?' I replied.

'He is obsessed with you, more like.' He marched on, taking his anger out on the muddy path.

'I think he is,' I replied, not diffusing the situation any. 'I was just saying that. Did you not hear me?'

'On his wedding day, he texts another woman? Pathetic. Bloody maracas. He's a weirdo.'

'I tried to tell you, Steve, but you never listen!'

I decided to leave Steve alone; he couldn't even be a friend, for all his protestations of love. I assumed Eric would back off.

All was settled for a while, and I found not being the object of their desire calming. Eric kept to 'band business' to start with, but a few months later, he came to visit.

'I'm unhappy,' he told me. He wasn't slim anymore but thin. 'I can't even eat! She wants children now, but I can't do that!'

'Why not?'

'I don't think I could cope,' he explained. 'And I don't want any child brought up like I was.' His father had left when he was young, and his mother was a tyrant.

'You don't need to be that kind of parent just because they were,' I told him.

'But I don't know how not to. It's all I've known.'

I wondered why this had not been discussed between them before. It irritated me. Unable to solve this problem, I sent him back to his wife.

Eric kept coming. He bought me gifts, more extravagant than before. Things he would have needed to send off-island for, so they must have arrived at their house first.

'Did Brenda see this?' I'd ask, bemused. I knew he was capable of secrets. I had started calling him Secret Squirrel as joke.

'Yes, she knows.'

'And she is okay with this?'

'She knows I like you.' This confused me further.

I did care for Eric. I thought he'd go away, but he was persistent. The most persistent man I've ever known. Lol and Susan both noticed he was hanging around again and questioned it at dinner one night.

'Yes, I like him, and he likes me,' I said.

'What does Brenda think about him coming around so much?' asked Susan

'She knows. She's fine about it,' I replied.

'Really?' Lol took a sip of her wine. 'So *he* says.'

'Yeah, I doubt that,' added Susan. 'I wouldn't be happy with Paul hanging around with another woman. I'd distance myself from him if I were you. It doesn't sound right.'

'I know he is off limits. I'm in control.' I tried to change the subject, but during dinner, he texted me unexpectedly.

'Oh, here we go. Let me guess ... Sir Text-a-Lot?' snorted Lol. 'Let's hear it, then.'

I read it out to them:

I've done it now—I've left her. Also bought a new drum kit.

'Well, at least he's put his money where his mouth is,' Lol said. He'd only been married a year. He moved in with his friend Duncan, and he came around a day later.

'I wish I'd never married her.' He'd say that often, along with reiterating not wanting children. 'In fact, I wish I'd never met her!' It seemed harsh given the ten plus years together.

'You are not impressing me, Eric. You shouldn't have got married in the first place. You told me all this before, and yet you still went ahead.'

'I know, but ... I've left her now. We can get together. It's you I want, and I know you want me,' he said as he approached me.

'No.'

'What?' He looked crestfallen.

'No! You need some time on your own to get yourself sorted out. I'll get the blame if you come straight to me. You could change your mind next week and go back to her. I need time to think.' I was strong.

A week later, I heard a knock at my door. My door was always open, and friends would come in and shout as they did. Some people locked their doors in the Isles, but I never did. Brenda was at the door.

'Can I come in? I need to speak to you.'

I made tea in the kitchen, and she didn't speak through the whole procedure, which seemed to take an inordinate amount of time. I took my tea through to the conservatory and sat down. Brenda refused the tea and didn't sit.

'What is going on?' she asked. I knew what she was talking about, and I was nervous at the confrontation, but this was my house, and I wasn't going to let her walk all over me.

'Regarding?'

'Eric,' she replied shortly.

'He's moved in with Duncan.' I stated the obvious.

'I don't understand what is going on.'

'He didn't explain?'

She got to the point. 'What is going on with you and Eric?'

'There is nothing going on with me and Eric.'

'Nothing?'

'Well, he is keen on me, has been for years. He is unhappy, and I listen.' I wished he was there. Since then, I try to get all parties in the room together if there is a disagreement. It saves people saying one thing to one and another thing to another. She looked at the picture on the wall, which he'd bought me.

'He gave me those things.' I gestured to the picture by way of explanation, not convinced she knew. I thought he had been Secret Squirreling these things to me.

'Yes, I know.'

'Well, you know then.'

'But why has he left now?'

I was brutal. I felt I was betraying him, but I was tired of it all. She had the nerve to come here, so she'd hear things she didn't want to hear. I hoped he had said them to her already.

'He told me he should not have married you. He didn't want to. He doesn't want children, and you do, so he left. He does like me, but there is no affair, which is what you are angling at. I've never laid a finger on him,' I summarised callously. Brenda didn't flinch.

'Yes. He said he didn't want children, but I don't want them just now.'

'He said you wanted five or six.'

'I'd like a large family. But it doesn't need to be right away. He'll change his mind.' She sounded sure this was going to happen. Not once did she seem out of control. She didn't shout or cry, her lips never trembled, her eyes were not moist. They were still dead, blank, and as hard as steel.

'You'll need to start sometime, love. But he seems adamant.' I felt more in control for a minute, but then she brought it back to me.

'But he chooses a woman with a child?' She squinted at me.

'We aren't together, Brenda. He didn't leave for me.'

She smirked at my response. Then she thought for a moment and asked, 'Did he tell you something about himself? Something that happened to him?'

I knew what she was referring to. I nodded, all the time looking her in the eye. She nodded back. I saw a flicker of reaction. After a clench of her teeth, she announced she was going.

She went without a look back, leaving the door wide open. I shut it and locked it immediately.

ERIC STAYED with his friend Duncan for three months. As Lol had said, he had put his money where his mouth was. It seemed like he had left her forever, so we did eventually get together. I was not *that* strong.

Of course, Brenda thought that this backed up her theory that I was involved. His mother and brother stopped speaking to him. I heard stories from my hairdresser of Brenda being ill, throwing up after drinking to excess. It made her seem more human than the version I was presented with from Eric. They thought I was to blame, and in their minds, it was now confirmed. Surely everyone knew he had been pursuing me for years, but that was forgotten.

Eric stayed at Duncan's until, after a while, I suggested he move in. He said it was too soon; however, he stayed with me most nights and used Duncan's house as a base. I believed that, over time, the drama would settle down. But it went on for a year. Over that time, he became irritated with things I did. I loaded the dishwasher too noisily. He refused to load it because he didn't live with me and they hadn't owned one. He still called the house he shared with Brenda 'home'.

I found out he was mean with money, and also mean on my behalf with my money. I started buying things in secret to avoid him checking the receipt and tutting. I stopped eating through lovesickness, stress, and dieting to keep my younger man. One night, I fainted on the stairs and fell to the bottom. I came to and climbed back up alone. He didn't even get up, despite hearing me fall.

'I was scared you were dead at the bottom of the stairs.' I felt like his concern was not for me but for how *he* would feel about it. Or was it something else?

Steve reacted badly to us getting together. He thought Eric was despicable for marrying Brenda and then dumping her. He went off the rails, stalking me, turning up wherever I was. Once, Steve's friend's wife approached me while I was singing and screamed, 'How can you show your face after what you did to Steve? Shut up! Shut up your stupid band!'

I never reacted.

Brenda grew friendly with Steve. He wouldn't speak to her as a rule, as she was a mere cleaner, and he thought himself an entrepreneur with grand ideas of marrying into wealth. However, it suited him to say I left him for Eric so they could both hate us together.

WHEN MY SISTER visited the island, we sat up drinking and talking. She quizzed Eric more than I ever had. She was always the brave, bold one. I never gave Eric a hard time, knowing the abuse he had suffered. He told her how sad he was about Brenda, and how she had wanted children and he hadn't, how terrible his brother and mum were to him, although they had started speaking again. (I didn't know that part.)

He told her his abuse story too. For a secret, he sure was telling a lot of people. My sister was sympathetic. Afterwards, he left the room to smoke a cigarette and for some space.

'Poor Eric. Oh my God, no wonder he is so edgy. What a terrible thing,' she said.

'What a shame,' I agreed.

After he came back in, and over another glass of wine, I decided to share my story. I didn't get the reaction I expected.

My sister didn't remember my abuse or The Man on holiday. She had no recollection at all! I tried to remind her she was there, and that I had saved her from him.

'Why do you have to make everything about you? I can't believe you're trying to get one-up on Eric here. This about Eric, not you.'

'It h-happened, though,' I managed to stutter.

'Why didn't you tell Mum then?' She rolled her eyes. She thought I was lying.

Eric shook his head and stared at the floor. He looked embarrassed and disappointed in me. He thought I was lying too, which was worse.

'I tried ...! It happened ...'

'Really, Angie? Or was *he* getting too much attention tonight?' She rolled her eyes. 'Fuck's sake. *I* need a fag now, Eric.' She looked appalled with me. They both stood up and went out for a cigarette, leaving me in the living room alone.

I was the wee girl again, realising there was no one to believe me. I was the single witness now, as the other witness not only couldn't remember but also thought I was making it up. Eric had said it once, and we all believed him. He was a strange one, quiet and nervy. Perhaps I was covering it all up too well. I looked like there was nothing wrong with me, so it sounded unreal. That was the last time I ever mentioned it. I made sure never to speak of it again.

Then came the news that Eric's father had been taken into hospital. Eric had had little contact with him over the years because Eric's mum hated her ex. Still, when Eric said he'd like to go see him, I advised him to go visit, and I agreed to go with him. Later, he came into the house and said I wasn't to go. Brenda had arranged to go with him. She wanted to see him too.

'When was this discussed?'

'Brenda phoned me at Duncan's when she found out.'

'And now you're going with your ex-wife instead of me?'

'Well, she knew him too. She says telling him we split up would be too much for him. I'm meeting her in the car park.'

'He doesn't know you split up?'

'No, I never told him. I don't see him often, as you know.'

'So he'd hardly care if you split up, would he?'

'I think it's best.'

I sat and fumed the entire evening. Eric stayed at Duncan's that night. Soon, we got the phone call that his dad had died. I asked about the funeral.

'About that ... I think it's best if you don't go,' Eric muttered.

'Why?'

'Mum is going, and my brother, of course, and it might be awkward.'

It hurt me, but I didn't make a fuss—his dad had just died, and the last thing I wanted was a scene. It was enough that his mother was going, knowing her hatred of the deceased. I didn't want her turning on me. But part of me thought we should face it out. I was struggling to control my irritation with these people who seemed to still control his life. Or maybe it was downright jealousy. After he came back from the funeral, I asked how it was.

'Brenda was there.'

'Oh, was she?'

'Mum brought her. She sat with the family at the front of the church.'

I was perturbed by this, but I thought I was being selfish. She had known his dad, so of course she would attend. But I had been barred from going, and that hurt.

Things were different after that. Instead of coming around all the time, Eric missed days and didn't answer his phone as quickly. He lost more weight. He said he was stressed and started talking to a counsellor, which I encouraged. Surely the counsellor could persuade him to release himself from the control he was under.

He told me the counsellor was texting him; he looked pleased. I thought it untoward, outwith sessions.

'Well, it is unusual, but I think she likes me—that's all I can say.' He laughed, as if it were a joke I wasn't in on. I felt like he'd transferred his feelings to another, and now I was the substitute Brenda, having to put up with his fantasy world of secrets.

Then one day, he didn't appear, and he didn't answer his phone. My cleaner came in the following day, a Tuesday, and told me she had spoken to Simone, Brenda's friend, who had told her Eric wanted to go back to Brenda. I felt as if I wasn't in the room as she babbled on about how he was over there right now but Simone had told Brenda not to take him back. I fretted for a few hours until he arrived to tell me.

'I'm going back to Brenda. She says I can't speak to you anymore.'

'What? Why?' I pleaded for an explanation.

'She is my wife.' He was like a robot.

'But they blamed me for the break-up. You knew that would happen. I took a huge risk on you. You said you didn't want her. You said you wished you'd never met her or married her. She wants children. What is happening?' I frantically listed all he had said, reminding him.

'She is my wife,' he said, more forcefully but still with no emotion.

'You said you didn't love her ...'

'She is my wife,' he repeated. And then one further explanation, 'I needed to get you out of my system.'

I swear he could have kicked me in the stomach and it wouldn't have hurt as much as his words did.

He moved back in with her on the Thursday. No apology nor any other explanation came. He was justified. It was all about what *he* needed.

He needed to pretend to leave her.

He needed to keep her on a string by faking living with his friend.

He needed to live a lie for over a year.

He needed to get me out of his system.

THIRTY-SIX

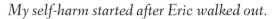

"My self-harm started after Eric walked out.

I cried and hit myself so hard I couldn't brush my hair for work the next day; the lumps and bruises on my head were so sore.

I was upset, angry for being stupid enough to believe him. I felt thoroughly deceived. All those times I felt jealous, I should have listened to my gut. Then I considered maybe Brenda had forced him to go back to her.

Did he make up her manipulative ways? Or was she the puppetmaster? I didn't know what was real and what wasn't.

The band split in the end, too, so I lost that as well. The fiddle player took Eric's side and started another band. Everything was taken away from me. He got to keep it all.

I tried to get over it. I had a child and a job to get up for. I kept going, but I was humiliated, hurt, and I felt dumb.

When my mask of happiness returned, I went out with a friend for a night. I was surprised to find I was enjoying myself. We moved onto the next bar, and I headed to the toilet while she bought drinks. When I returned, she hustled me out of the door. 'I'll explain later.'

'What the hell?' I asked.

'She was there. Brenda, with Simone.'

'So what? We live on the same island. I can't avoid her forever,' I said.

'While you were in the loo, Simone told me that when you came back she was going to pour a drink over you. Said she would glass your face.'

'Then I'd call the Police.' I was angry at her dictating what I did.

'She said if it wasn't for you, Eric and Brenda would have been fine. None of this would have happened.'

I got the entire blame. Part of me wished I had had a secret affair. I had tried to be upfront and open. I should have been as devious as Eric was. I bet Brenda wouldn't have minded. She was sick from the embarrassment alone. I always thought the cheater was the bad guy, but Eric didn't have to face any consequences.

I was groomed, duped into having an affair that wasn't at all secret. It was all in public, for all to see, and still, I was the one at fault.

He got the affair he wanted in the guise of leaving her. It was a grand and perfect manipulation from beginning to end. A well-played game that he won.

That's when I had my breakdown.

Third Section—Island

- Eric
- Brenda
- Simone
- Steve

Industrial estate, cliff, doll, spa

THIRTY-SEVEN

'HIYA.' I hear a singsong voice. Preston is in the kitchen before I can turn around.

I'm looking out the kitchen window, watching Preston's mum and brother preparing to leave. He gazes out the window with me, and we both watch in silence as they reverse out to depart. His mum looks up in the direction of Preston's kitchen window, not mine, but we both jump back together, thinking she could see us. We grab onto each other and laugh uproariously.

'God help me.' He rolls his eyes and heads to the kettle.

'How was that, then?' I enquire as he prepares two mugs.

'Usual ... hellish.' He doesn't look up from his business.

'Crème brûlée,' I suggest. This stops him, and he dreamily looks into the distance and smiles.

'Yeah, crème brûlée. Cross me, cross the road!' Preston smirks as he dunks the tea bags.

I consider this, realising I don't understand what he means. 'What's this now?' I wonder out loud.

'Cross me, cross the road, as I've always said,' he explains, carrying the mugs over to the table.

'Never actually heard you say that ever,' I argue. 'Does that mean one has to get to the other side of the road to get away from you? Or is it a suggestion for someone to go get hit by a lorry?'

'It's as dangerous to cross the road as crossing me.' He speaks as if he is explaining it to a child.

'I've not been run over yet, so it's pretty safe to cross you then,' I suggest.

He glares and pouts at me and replies, 'Fuck's sake! Do you need to dissect everything?'

He is prickly today. I try to cheer him up, as I can see he is bothered by this last visit.

'So, what's his name then? The brother. Big bro...? Let me guess. What household item is he named after, or is it a place? Is he called Kirk? Because he was born in Falkirk? Peter? Because you have an uncle in Peterhead? Or Fraser? Your parents once took a coach trip to Fraserburgh? Or Dom? Mum looked under the sink one day at the bleach, saw Domestos, and that was her mind made up?'

'Red,' he answers. He pouts and sips his tea with his arm across his body. I think he is angry, until he raises his eyebrows and nods. He is challenging me to keep guessing.

'Red things, red things ... Is it because he was conceived in Redcar? Or did your mum get a craving for Reddy Brek when she was pregnant?' I laugh at my own cleverness.

He pauses and waits while I flounder to think of more red things. He gestures for me to keep guessing.

'Red, red...' I struggle.

'No!' He interrupts. 'His hair is red,' he exclaims incredulously. 'Did you not notice?' He rolls his eyes and then laughs, knowing that was too obvious, but he appreciates me trying. 'You two ready to go?'

'Nearly. I just need a couple of things for the plane.'

I am going to visit Susan and Paul on the island. Callum is coming along, as his father still lives there, so they will spend some time together while I have the week to myself.

I pull my sparkly notebook out from under the newspaper while

Preston isn't looking and slip it into my handbag. Preston drives us both to the airport to jump on the 'flying tractor'—my name for the propeller plane, making the last flight.

PAUL PICKS me up from the tiny airport, and we drop Callum at his dad's house before heading to Paul and Susan's place overlooking the sea. I'm given a light supper, as it's late, and we talk of times past and catch up on island gossip. Who left whom? Who is dating whom?

We talk of Steve, who died two days ago in a car accident. I saw on the news that someone had died, but they hadn't named him until I got off the plane. Susan told me, once I was settled with a brandy. He'd never met the ideal woman with the major prospects. Instead, he had a fling with his teenage neighbour and got her pregnant. There was no one else on the road; he took the bend too fast. The child will be very wealthy.

I speak of work and how things are now with Callum and John. Cancer never comes up, thank God. They are the perfect hosts. They both work, however, so I will be left to my own devices most of the time. I prefer this to someone fussing over me every minute. We make plans for tomorrow evening: dinner at the local curry house.

Eric and Brenda don't come up in conversation this time either. I haven't heard anything interesting about Eric and Brenda for at least ten years. It's a small island in many ways, but it seems some circles don't overlap. I stopped asking about them a while back, as there never was anything to tell. Susan would say, 'It's funny, they still live in the town, I think, but I never hear anything of them. I never see them either. No one seems to know anything about them.'

THIRTY-EIGHT

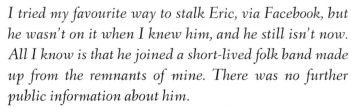

" I tried my favourite way to stalk Eric, via Facebook, but he wasn't on it when I knew him, and he still isn't now. All I know is that he joined a short-lived folk band made up from the remnants of mine. There was no further public information about him.

Eric's mum and brother showed little of interest on their profiles—no mention of grandchildren or nieces and nephews. But Brenda could have the six she wanted by now if Eric changed his mind as she predicted.

I found Brenda's profile easily enough. Her profile picture was, and still is, their wedding photo. I'd have thought it might be a painful memory, considering all that happened after, but she is still perpetuating the myth of her fairy tale.

A lot of her posts are private, but I found some photos. The most recent photo of Eric, taken about eighteen months ago, told quite a story. He was sitting with their new addition—an electric drum kit. Surely if *you can put up a photo of a 'new addition' drum kit, any 'new addition' children would be mentioned.*

The house looked cluttered, more than I could ever stand. Books, CDs, and magazines were lying on the table and the floor. On the bookshelves to one side sat a fruit bowl filled with batteries and elastic bands. Pens, envelopes, and papers were stacked up on a side table with a handle missing.

Eric has lost his boyish looks. He was handsome enough to get away with being a bit odd when he was younger. His pain shows on his face now. His mouth twists into a gummy sneer rather than a smile. Folds of skin wrinkle his neck. The poison within is now showing without. I can barely see what I considered handsome back then.

The most noteworthy thing was that they possessed an amazing collection of dolls. A whole wall of them! I wondered if they were trying to be quirky on purpose, to make them more interesting than they are. All those dull-eyed dolls staring out made me shudder. Apart from the creepy dolls, I saw no toys, no children. Are the dolls the substitutes? I suddenly knew what Brenda had given up to get him back.

Had he persuaded her, on his part, with the inheritance money from his father to buy the bigger house? I once considered Brenda kept him prisoner, making excuses for him being trapped in the relationship. He had never wanted children, and he managed to get out of that by leaving, using it as a bargaining chip. He got what he wanted from me and what he wanted from her in the end. She went down in my estimation then. That was what saved her.

I was glad I didn't end up with Eric when I saw his gurning face in the photo. Plus, I couldn't live with the

*mess in that house. I should trap him in there and set fire
to it, but that would spark a lot of investigation.*

THERE IS no need for me to be here in particular, but I have a reason to walk this road, since it joins one main road to another. I'm out for a bloody walk if anyone asks. I could know anyone along here, or I could be passing through.

I had tried to find the new house soon after Eric left me, but I stopped myself. I have none of this control now.

It is further from the centre of town than Susan's place, nearly on the outskirts. I can't case the house all day like a stakeout, waiting for them to appear, but I know roughly where it is. I assume he hasn't changed jobs, so I know the route he would likely take.

I leave suburbia and pop over to the hotel where Brenda used to work as a cleaner. I don't expect to see her, but I'm ready, just in case. At reception, I try to make an appointment to get a facial with the beautician there this week. The phone lines at reception are down, so the reception staff send me downstairs to make it in person.

I make my way down and wait for someone to come around the partition and serve me, as it is deserted out front. Simone walks around the corner, takes one look at me, and marches back around the partition. She does not return. I call after her half-heartedly. Then I head back to the main reception.

'Can I speak to the manager, please?' I complain to management about being refused service. They seem confused, trying to call down before remembering the phone lines aren't working. The manager asks me to come down with her to sort this out.

'No thanks. I wanted to let you know she refused to serve me. She was very rude. I'll go to the beautician in the High Street.'

As I leave, I see Brenda plodding around the corner, dragging a bin bag. *Oh, the glamour.* She doesn't see me, but Simone will tell her

I'm here. I make a note of the time, hoping she has regular hours. The High Street beautician has space for me in two days.

THE NEXT DAY, Paul and Susan go to work after breakfast. Paul is working at the hotel today, fitting carpets. I wonder whether he will hear anything about my complaint about Simone. Holding my cup of tea, I stare out the window, gazing at the sea till late morning.

Summer is the best time to visit the island, but it gives no indication of the island's moods in the winter. I make a decision to go for a walk later, but then I can't quite believe my eyes when Eric walks right past the window. I grab my coat and head after him. It's a straight road down to the town, with no turns off, so I have a clear view of him. I check the time.

He takes a harbour walk to his job at the garage in the industrial estate—nothing has changed in all this time. I could push him into the harbour, but there are too many people around, and he could climb out, unless he got trapped between boats.

I follow him, watching him from the back. He walks like an undertaker, all solemn and upright. He must be on a mid/late shift today. I work out roughly when he might return. Later, I tell Susan I needed a breath of air, which she lets go without questioning. I'm a cancer victim; sometimes I need space.

I take a walk and sit on a bench where I know I will get a clear view of him coming. It's 7.30pm. I wait some time, hoping he hasn't taken another route. Then I see him in the distance, walking the same route home.

I have time to stare. He has a defensive look, unsmiling. His head is still, but his eyes dart from side to side. He is alert to danger, looking for predators. His eyes are sunken quite deep above his high cheekbones, but his furrowed brows and the dark circles under his eyes increase the effect. The eyes flicking back and forth remind me of something. Perhaps a gunslinger? No. It is *Eagle-Eyes Action Man*

—I always wanted one of those, but it wasn't a girl's toy. I might get one off eBay and call it Eric.

I step out, standing in his way. I can tell he feels trapped; I can almost smell his sweat. Eric keeps walking, his lips tightening.

He will love the intrigue of this! I stuff a note into his pocket as he passes. He always acted like a slippery spy. Secret Squirrel! I nearly forgot I called him that—ah, fond memories.

Eric smirks and reddens, but he doesn't break stride. He'll read it in his shed away from her. Wouldn't anyone at least read it? He won't throw it away. He may be honest, maybe even show Brenda, but nothing will come of it, and they'll laugh about it. Still, I am confident that will not occur.

I tell Paul and Susan I feel better for the fresh air, and we drink wine and chat far too late into the night on a weeknight.

THIRTY-NINE

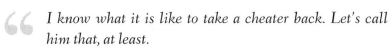

" I know what it is like to take a cheater back. Let's call him that, at least.

I didn't think Eric was cheating at the time. As far as I knew, they were finished. But HE knew he was cheating. He was always going to go back. Some people claim that a relationship which survives cheating is stronger than it was before. I doubt that.

I try to analyse what happened. I have spent a lot of time doing this, and I still have no set answers. Cheaters fall into a few categories.

Was he emotionally immature? Out for fun? I rule those out. It was all too intense for that.

Was he neglected and became resentful when he felt ignored? I have considered this possibility over the years. He certainly had little favourable to say about Brenda; however, I'm certain those were all lies to gets his needs met. He got all he wanted from both of us.

He must have told her it was all my fault. Simone said if it wasn't for me, they would have been fine. It *must help Brenda to think that, rather than swallow the unpalatable truth that her husband is a sexual sociopath.*

If someone promises fidelity and goes behind your back, if they are prepared to look into the eyes and lie to you, intentionally hurt you deeply and destroy everything, then they are surely not worth it. Is it like this for Brenda? It's a rare person who can trust again after being dishonoured by a cheat. Mistrust replaces the secure, solid bond you had together. Instead, the relationship hangs by a fragile thread that struggles to support the weight of doubt and may snap at any time.

THE NOTE SIMPLY READ, 'On the island for two days—call me' and included my phone number. I worry about phone records if he takes me up on my offer, but who'd be checking? My phone buzzes at 6am. It's him. I leave it till Susan and Paul go to work.

Hi. How are you? His text begins.

I see him pass the window. He has worked out where I am staying. He knows where my friends live from years ago, although they don't know anything about him now. He looks in, and I stare out.

I text him about ten minutes later, when he might be arriving at the industrial estate. He mentions he reached work at that second so can't text till after six or on his lunch break. *Thank you for that information.*

How's Brenda? Is she working today?

At work now, but she'll be in later.

I figured as much. The same shifts as yesterday and the day before.

Certain they will both be out, I boldly stride up to their door and knock on it. Of course, no one answers, so I try around the back, in case they didn't hear me. I check the back door. As I hoped, the door opens.

I examine the doll collection. Brenda mentioned on Facebook that her favourite was called Erica. I find the doll and remove its head, placing it at its feet. *There's your child substitute.*

My phone buzzes, which makes me jump, so I get out of there.

Eric and I text back and forth during his lunch break. No wonder Lol used to call him Sir Text-a-Lot.

Hey there, Secret Squirrel x

Hey, Angie!

I'm only here for a short time. Can we meet up?

Yeah, why not? X

In the afternoon, I head for my facial to relax. I couldn't imagine Simone doing this for me. Later, after dinner and a lot of wine with Susan and Paul, I text Eric again.

At the car park behind the wee white church, tomorrow at 10.30?

I'm meant to be working

Our little secret, old times sake. No one will know x

Ok, Cool. I'll make sure no one knows. Also I burnt the note.

Our secret x

Our secret x

FORTY

"I wonder whether I should wear gloves. I doubt it matters.

I'll take along a flask of sugary tea with strong medication mixed in—my anxiety and depression drugs, a sleeping pill, painkillers, and a little antihistamine for good luck. Basically, enough to knock him out, but all quite readily available medications and some things he might take already.

I'll also take a blanket. I'll explain to him that it's in case anyone comes along. I can cover myself up and hide. He will agree that's a good idea, while he sips a cup of tea.

I'll pretend to drink the tea, too, mentioning the plastic cup makes it taste a bit funny. Knowing him, he'll swallow some more to check.

If we see a dog walker, I'll hide under the blanket, slide down in the seat. If the dog walker is ever asked about the guy in the car, he'll say Eric was on his own.

It's the perfect cover for a pretend affair—and for a murder.

THE NEXT DAY, Eric meets me in his car at the assigned quiet place. He'd called in sick to work. It couldn't work better for me. He never apologises or mentions what happened all those years before. It's as if nothing at all occurred.

Eric doesn't mention Brenda. He rambles on about random 'music talk' and his work, particularly a woman he believes fancies him there. He had bought her a gift and thought about getting a T-shirt with her face on it. Clearly, he is a big fan.

He always was all talk and little action. I reckon that's why the counsellor was such a hit with him. Eric likes to talk, and he does so all the way to the beauty spot by the cliffs.

FORTY-ONE

ERIC IS UNCONSCIOUS NOW. The handbrake is on, and I move his right foot, heavy onto the accelerator to hold it down. His left is on the clutch. I put the car in first gear and then remove Eric's foot from the clutch. I release the handbrake and stumble out the passenger side, remembering to take the flask, the blanket, and Eric's phone, in case any of my messages are still on there. I place them all on top of my backpack. The car moves a little, or at least feels like it will move.

I double-check that there is no one around. I can see for miles in all directions. I open the driver door. The car feels precarious. We are about twenty feet from the edge; that alone makes my knees feel like jelly. I never liked cliffs or driving near them. Driving in harbour areas is unpleasant for me too. Whenever I was dropping anyone off at the pier, I always felt anxious.

My scarf flaps in the wind. I take it off and stick it up my hoodie. It is the height of summer, and it's still windy here. I roll the car nearer the edge; if I time it wrong, he could fall out the bloody door if I don't have time to shut it. I reach in and start the ignition, immediately jumping back and shutting the door. The car takes off, the door not quite shut. Eric wavers about in the seat. I turn away. I don't wait to see what happens next.

It's a workout, and I'm also struggling to cope emotionally. What if someone sees me with him in the car? I sing to hide any sound.

Taking up his phone, I turn it off and stamp on it. I keep it with me in my rucksack, along with my blanket and flask to dispose of later.

I didn't bring my own phone in case it's used to locate me, although I don't know how that works. It's a fair way to the small, quaint fishing village on the island that I'm heading for. I'll say I went for the day. From my planning, I know it's about six miles away—easy enough for me, as I always liked long walks. This is different, however. I need to get away from the scene, not wander around admiring the scenery.

The walk helps clear my head. I cross over fields to avoid being noticed from the road, but then I wonder whether a woman rambling over the fields looks more suspicious. No one goes out walking around here as a rule. I could go for miles and not see a soul, but I feel more exposed here, in the countryside. No trees punctuate the miles of open space. I traverse farmland I don't know the name of. It feels like longer than six miles without landmarks to break up the minutes. If I'm seen, a walk is a walk. I don't want to seem like I'm frantic or hurrying, but I am.

Later, I can blame the cancer for my extreme tiredness. I'll say that walking helps me mentally, but I overdid it. I'll admit to a five-mile walk but insist I circled around the town.

I decide to head away from the coast, go inland across the fields, avoiding the farm buildings and taking me past the reservoir.

I head uphill; from here, I can see the town at last. It's another mile until I reach the town perimeter. That takes me to the imaginatively named Top Road, where a car drives past. I jump. *That is a witness. But to what? A woman on the edge of town, unrelated to the poor guy who drove himself off a cliff.* I'm just a woman walking along a street.

I cut through the school to reach the narrow winding streets of the equally imaginatively named Main Street. Composing myself, I notice that the houses are close together here; it makes me feel safer. There are signs of life—all carrying on as normal. They don't know what I know.

I enter a café and order a cup of tea. I pop into all the shops I can. It could be a fine thing to be seen. Of course, I'm here two hours after the event, and I don't have an alibi, but I hope no one can remember what time of day I passed by.

I wander around to the Travel Centre at the pierhead to catch the bus. It isn't due yet, so I nip into the pub and down a large whiskey. It goes straight to my head.

I use their toilets, not decorated since the 1980s by the look of it, and I am about to leave when I realise I left my rucksack in the public bar. It has Eric's phone in there. I race back, but I can't see it. *Where is it?*

'This what you are looking for?' The barman dangles my backpack.

'I forgot my bag,' I say, stating the obvious.

No more booze! I must concentrate.

My mouth is dry with the sour taste of panic, but I gulp it down on the bus back to Paul and Susan's house. They aren't home yet, so I run through to the garage and hammer that phone into a hundred pieces.

FORTY-TWO

News of the sad loss of life off the cliffs broke after Susan and Paul left for work. The cliffs are the first place to be checked when someone goes missing here, especially in a car.

Comments are already peppering social media, a lot prefaced with, 'I didn't know him, but ...'

No one will look for his phone, which will presumably be thought to be at the bottom of the sea. It's actually in pieces inside a freezer bag in my backpack. But I still can't have it in my possession.

I'll pop out for a walk after, drop pieces of the phone in several bins around town. Some of it is dust, so I'll sprinkle that into the harbour.

On my return, I'll clean out the flask again—a lot. There is so much to remember. I don't want to knock myself out next time I go for a picnic.

I feel like I'm about to have a panic attack. It's because I am on an island. I am trapped. I never felt like that all those years ago, but now ...

I GATHER my wits and meet Lol and Susan in the pub for lunch, as arranged.

'No wonder he did it, living with her. He was always strange, though. What a pair.' Lol is in full flow with wine in hand. They are sharing a bottle, but I'm having tea after my episode with the whiskey.

'Yeah. I'm not really wanting to talk about it,' I say. I'm not sure how to play it. I never talked well of him to them after he left me, so I can't start singing his praises now. Similarly, I don't want to sound too glad about it either.

I let her talk. She goes back to the subject she was told not to cover.

I say, 'I never saw him for years. He disappeared into the shadows.'

Susan joins in the same line of questioning. 'Yes, but he was always lurking. Lurkio you called him, Lol, remember?'

'I called him many things,' Lol interjects between sips of wine.

'He was stalking you at that wedding, remember that?' mentions Susan.

'Yes,' I reply.

'And they never had the kids she wanted. He was the man-child for that house, but she was boss overall, I think,' Lol muses. 'I'll tell you what I think. I think she will take this in her stride. Hard as nails, her. That day she came to see you—very cool and calm and steely.'

'Yes, she was.' I hadn't thought about her reaction.

Lol continues. 'And then able to take him back, after all that. You told her what he said about her. She knew he stalked you for ages, bought you things. I'd never have allowed that. I'd have killed him.'

'Mmmm. *Steely*—that's the word,' I agree, hoping they stop talking about this soon.

'His mum and brother were funny ones as well,' says Susan, keeping it going.

'The whole lot of them are odd. I haven't seen him for years either. He was always excellent at skulking about, though, big Lurkio,' snorts Lol as she takes another gulp of wine mid-sentence.

Not one person is questioning what happened. It's as plain as day. It's a well-known spot for this sort of thing. I hope the police don't ask too many questions, but anyone they ask will say he was weird anyway—'He was never right, that boy.' Small towns, eh?

'Did you see him?' Lol asks randomly, bringing me smack-bang back into the present. I don't think I visibly jump, but I feel like I'm twitching inside.

'When?'

'While you were up this time?'

'Not since that Tuesday he walked out on me. But I'm not saying he never saw me.' I risk a joke about how he used to sneak about. *Oh boy, I've become him.*

Lol wears a wry smile. 'Yeah. Actually, when I think about it, I always thought he thought too much of himself to ... you know,' she muses. Susan nods.

I open my mouth to mention the anxiety drugs in the flask, then I close it again. *Hell, no need to give the game away.*

I excuse myself. I sit sweating in the toilets. I hyperventilate. Some tears come. When I go back, it's obvious I have been crying. I am red in the face and have been gone far too long.

'Are you okay? It's a big shock,' Susan says.

'I don't know why I'm crying. I haven't cared about him in years, but ...'

They both nod understandingly.

'... we had some good times.' I throw that in, but I miss out on saying *before he got obsessed and lied and schemed and wrecked everything.*

I take a sip of tea but struggle to swallow it. It's okay that I cried, but I hope nobody else sees it. I don't want people to make any connection between Eric and me. Most will have forgotten that episode a long time ago, but Lol and Susan won't be the only ones who remember.

I STAY ANOTHER NIGHT, and then I pick up Callum on the drive to the airport. I feel relieved by the separation of distance.

We arrive back in the flat, and I start to unpack when I hear my son shout from his bedroom.

Rats Domino is lying still and cold at the bottom of his cage. I'm sure I told Preston to feed him while we were away. His food is there, so he did as I asked, and it's not my fault. It's obvious he has died of old age. We wrap him up and put him in a box in the kitchen.

Callum cleans the cage out solemnly. 'It was just a rat,' I keep saying, but I feel anxiety building and I wash down some beta-blockers with a brandy. At least I know the cat is safe at the cattery.

In bed, I keep imagining there was no food in his cage and that I must have forgotten to tell Preston. I am to blame. I hit myself twice. I kick the covers off.

I can't check the cage now, as it's all cleaned out. Why didn't I get Callum to leave it as it was until morning so that I could check it?

No, I tell myself, *there was food there. It wasn't my fault! I'm sure.* Or I think I'm sure.

However, I still can't sleep. A voice in my head keeps repeating: *You killed the rat. You killed the rat.*

Third Section—Island

- ~~Eric cliff~~
- ~~Brenda doll~~
- ~~Simone work~~
- ~~Steve dead~~

Industrial estate, doll, spa

Fourth Section—Perthshire

- Kate
- Tom
- Chris
- Michael—radio station
- Douglas—council
- Paddy
- Linda—monkey
- Denise—monkey
- Mandy—monkey
- Gillian the slut
- Sandra—beauty queen
- Barbara—the next one

FORTY-THREE

"Paddy hated me at 'Hello'. I did not know at the time, but he was incapable of love. He admired me perhaps or saw what he wanted to be in me. Or saw what he could get from me.

Can't get worse than that last guy I went out with, I'd thought. I underestimated myself. I can always go one better.

He studied me and sucked me in, with the intention of cutting me off at the knees and leaving me emotionally dead. What he admired soured and became envy; what he didn't like, my flaws and insecurities, he used against me like weapons.

He kicked me off the pedestal he had put me on at the beginning, and I spent all my time trying to claw my way back onto it with his foot on my head.

FORTY-FOUR

'WHAT DON'T you like about yourself, and how would you improve yourself?' Paddy asked me on our first date. I thought it an interesting question. I know now he was fishing for clues, seeking my Achilles heel.

Paddy had approached me on Facebook chat after a gig. I didn't know him, but we had several mutual friends. His profile gave little away: single, liked bowls, folk and jazz music. My friends vaguely knew him as a quiet chap whose wife left him almost ten years previously and who lived with his two children. He seemed a bit cheeky, but not rough or rude. Eight years older than me and not model-like like Eric, Paddy was bald and chubby—an ordinary guy. He had baggage, but so did I.

He told me his wife, Monica, had left him after an affair. He didn't go out with anyone for many years but had a couple of dates with the local glamour-puss just last year. He joked she was high maintenance, which I could believe.

'I wish I could calmly accept it when things don't go to plan. I get anxious and sometimes angry. It's anxiety—a mental illness—so I don't think it can fully be changed, more managed.'

I half learnt, after the breakdown, that I could recognise my gut reactions and deal with them most of the time. But after I lost my temper, I could also see when my emotions had taken over. I hoped to get better at controlling myself.

'I don't believe in mental illness,' he said. 'Sure, people can get down, but that's just a feeling. It shouldn't affect your actions.'

I tried to explain it more, but he shook his head and laughed. 'No, no, no ... you are in charge of your own mind.'

I changed the subject.

I told him my insecurities about being liked, about being a people-pleaser. I thought it would make us better together if I shared. I wasn't the person on the pedestal or the stage, but a regular human being with worries.

I thought I was being brave, but Paddy saw the weaknesses. I didn't know it, but I had given him the ammunition to destroy me.

I spoke about how I couldn't stand infidelity and lies, not after my last experience. He agreed, as the same thing had happened to him. I felt we had something in common. He understood how it felt to have someone deceive you, to live a double life.

He asked if I believed in God. I didn't know why he brought that up. Maybe he knew I went to church. I did; He didn't. I didn't think it was a big deal. It wasn't at the beginning.

'We'll just agree to disagree on that,' I said and smiled.

'Yeah,' he nodded.

I'd moved away from the island and the gossips there by then. The relentless intimidation was tearing me apart. They wouldn't let it go, and I needed to.

I STARTED ANEW IN PERTHSHIRE. I liked my house and my job, and Callum was doing well at school.

I worked with a man called Chris, although I didn't see or speak to him often. He seemed aloof, arrogant even, and he ignored me most of the time.

A man named Tom started with us when I didn't want to increase my hours to full time. Tom seemed easygoing and quiet. As a single mother, I didn't go to the staff nights out; instead, I sat in the house, minding my own business.

I planned to live quietly, and then no one would want to throw drinks over me in pubs. I was thirty-seven and needed to calm things down. I seemed to attract trouble—or maybe I went looking for it. I considered it all might be my fault, so I took myself out of the equation.

The girls at work would come in with stories of staff nights out, about Chris being a sexist pig and Tom sleeping with staff members. The stories didn't add up to Tom's persona at work. He was soft-spoken, diligent, and training for further qualifications. The thought of him being a womaniser made me laugh. He was a funny-looking guy, not at all attractive to me. He was short, fat and hairy every-where from what I could see. Thick, curly dark hair sprouted up from his collar and his ears. His eyebrows met underneath thick glasses. He seemed ten years older instead of ten years younger than me.

The boss, or Bossman as I called him, was a flamboyant Glaswe-gian who was away most of the time. On one visit, he announced that we were expanding, so a new girl would come in part-time.

Kate worked in a similar job in the next town, and he had heard she would be a positive addition to the team.

She'd led a perfect life. Her rich mummy and daddy loved her, and she had all she wanted. She was attractive, if not beautiful, although a little long in the face and with too pointed a chin to be the model Bossman described her as. But she was tall, and, more impor-tantly, slim, with flowing, white-blonde hair.

Tom's head was turned. He described her as a 'breath of fresh air' as soon as she walked through the door. I raised my eyebrows. *Here comes trouble*, I thought. Little did I know to what extent.

I had come out of hiding after a while and started singing again. I deserved a social life, after all. I enjoyed it and I made some friends. This time, I'd manage things better. I was still wary, but my guard lowered.

When Paddy saw me at my happiest, singing and getting all the attention in the room, he must have thought this was the life he needed to experience. However, he didn't like any of my friends, so we didn't hang out with them. I had to spend time with them on my own.

Over time, any solid support network I had, or anything that made me secure, Paddy attacked. He kept his friends. He barely kept in contact with his two male friends from school, but then he had the 'flying monkeys'—the gossipy, back-up bitches. This harem of female witches had rallied around him when his wife left.

The leader of the gang, the 'main monkey', was Linda. She was Monica's cousin who had taken Paddy's side against her relative. She had always been jealous of her pretty cousin, and now she possessed an ally in Paddy. He told me once that Linda did not love her husband. He announced that with no explanation.

'How do you know?'

'She told me. We were out walking one day. And she told me.'

'You were walking with another man's wife and she told you she didn't love her husband?' I wondered under what set of circumstances that could occur, but that was all the information he gave me. He wanted me to think she loved him instead. Maybe she did, and that was why she didn't like me. Maybe that information was how Paddy commanded a hold over her.

Then there was Mandy, his ally in the divorce. She was the wife of Monica's coworker, the man Monica had left Paddy for. She had reason to hate Monica as well, and they had the deception in common. Maybe she fancied the ultimate revenge of being in Monica's place. Paddy hinted at that too.

Denise, the fat local hotelier, was the cleverest of them. A physical mess due to cigarettes and booze, Paddy often mentioned that she hadn't

THE BUCKET LIST   185

always been like that. She'd been a 'looker' once. He'd wink and hint at her, too, but I always laughed at that. The woman struggled to walk a hundred yards without wheezing and coughing and leaning on her stick.

Together, the flying monkeys would keep the positive word going about Paddy. They'd all feel sorry for him. They'd all be happy for him to meet someone new.

'If only he could meet someone decent,' they'd say ... until he met them. Then they would lap up all his negative stories, believe the girl wasn't good enough (perhaps because they wanted to be that girl), and spread it around all over again.

I met all his friends officially when we were invited to Denise's wedding anniversary party. I was kept away from them after that, apart from the odd accidental meeting in passing. He kept me from his family too; I saw his two kids four times, and his father and brother once in four years. There were never any joint Christmas or birthday celebrations. He couldn't chance me correcting the picture he had painted of me.

Before I headed to the anniversary party, my phone pinged and Paddy's name popped up. I was nervous about meeting his friends. It was our first outing as a couple in front of them all.

No words were in the message. It was just a post from Facebook mocking people who believed in God as moronic, sky-fairy-believing idiots. I didn't answer. I tried to forget it. It was such a small thing. It didn't matter.

At the party, Paddy joked to the flying monkeys that I bossed him about, how he was a bit scared of me. His friends smiled, but they looked me up and down. I guessed they assumed that was how it was. After all, why wouldn't they? He said it right in front of me.

After the party, we had some more drinks at my place. 'Why did you send that message?' I asked him.

'What message?'

'About God.' He laughed, and when I didn't laugh in return, he rolled his eyes.

'Don't start. It was just a joke. I should have known you wouldn't get it. I thought it was funny.'

Just a joke! He should have known I wouldn't like it, and he did know. He did it to knock me down a bit before the party. I thought that if I explained I didn't like it, he wouldn't do it again. Instead, I gave him another tool to get at me. We'd agreed to disagree, and he knew then it was a provocative device.

'Okay, doesn't matter. It's a weird thing to send to someone who believes in God.'

I always had since I was a child. I would speak to Him and tell Him all my secrets, although He knew them already. God never let me down. His job is to love unconditionally, and that is the point. He never judges and always forgives all your sins. Only people let you down and hold grudges over nothing. But then ... what was I doing? No, mine aren't nothing! And, you know the Bible does say, 'an eye for an eye'.

'Why did you tell them I bullied you?'

'What now? I was only joking.' He looked a little irritated.

'Is it funny to make stuff up about me, like I'm a bitch, in front of people?' I half laughed.

'I was just joking. You know, a joke?'

'They will think it's a joke, but they might think it's true too. I mean, you can joke about my real quirks that are ridiculous, there are plenty to choose from, but not things I've never done. Please don't do that.' I laughed half-heartedly.

Paddy was quiet through all of this until I told him not to do it again. Then he stood up, towering over me. 'I'm walking on eggshells with you and your behaviour.'

'My behaviour?' I was bewildered, searching for something I had done wrong.

'Everyone can see it. The way you treat people.' I was confused. His accusation had no relevance to anything that had gone before.

'How do I treat people?'

He didn't answer. I now know he said nothing because he had no example of how I treated people, but him saying it had made me stop. I'd told Paddy I wanted to improve myself, and he was watering that seed of doubt in me.

'If you can't accept me as I am, I should leave. We are over,' he announced. I was shocked that something so small had triggered this response. Paddy was ready to walk out of my life forever, pausing at the door, looking back at me.

'Goodbye.' The door slammed.

He was outside for a matter of minutes. Then he stormed back in. 'Do you want this to be over?' he asked.

'You're the one who left,' I reminded him.

'Maybe we can give things another go?'

'Okay,' I murmured, thinking we had overdone the booze. Things would be better in the morning. I should have locked the door as soon as he walked out.

FORTY-FIVE

Paddy often told me he was a philosopher and a poet who came up with exceptional ideas. I saw no evidence of it, but he liked to talk.

He often talked in the third person, marvelling at his own cleverness, in awe of his own magical genius. 'I just thought it. It really is amazing how I can just think these things. It's a tremendous talent. It must mean something. I mean, it doesn't just come from nowhere. Paddy must have an amazing brain.'

It was all said with a smile and a laugh, and I'd find him funny. I didn't know he believed it all. He didn't believe in God, but perhaps that was because he thought he was God.

He was the opposite of me. I doubted every thought and feeling I ever experienced. No amount of discussion or facts would cast a shred of doubt on anything that crossed Paddy's mind. He'd debate for hours. He loved to.

I was no fan of small talk, so I entertained this until

I learnt it was code for, 'Let me deliberately say provocative things so I can get the fight I want.' In actuality, all debate was him talking.

He had several stock ideas and stories that I heard so many times I could have recited them. I learnt not to contradict him.

Alarm bells were ringing, and I should have listened. He'd often say that before his mother died, she thought him the most beautiful child. He would call himself the 'lady charmer' and talk about his amazing charisma and attractiveness. It was funny, very funny for a guy who'd had only a couple of dates since his wife left him ten years ago.

I once shared a Facebook meme about mental health. It was about how cancer victims are never blamed for getting cancer, so mentally ill people shouldn't be blamed for being mentally ill. Nothing offensive, I thought.

At first, he didn't answer texts. I asked him why he wasn't answering. When he did answer, I got a tirade.

'How dare you belittle cancer victims?' It was an unexpected question. 'You can't compare them to mental people. They are in control of their own heads, for God's sake.'

'It was just a meme. I had a breakdown after ...' I tried to explain how he had the wrong end of the stick. For the cleverest man in the universe, he was a little slow.

'Yeah, I know ... Eric dumped you. When my wife left me, I was down and sad about it too, but I never made out I was ill,' he raged.

'The point was that people with mental illness should get more empathy, not be told to "get over it". You'd never say that to someone with an illness like *cancer. It's an illness, like chemicals in the brain.' I thought if I just spelt it out ...*

'The hell it is.' He had warned me he didn't believe in mental illness when we met. He thought anyone claiming mental illness was nothing but an attention-seeker. Therefore, so was I.

I knew for sure his anger during this episode was personal when his flying monkey Mandy shared the same post and he 'liked' it. Religion and mental illness, were continual niggles, but the next episode with Paddy pushed me over the edge.

BACK AT WORK, I heard Tom and Kate had got together on a course and were now a perfect couple. The staff he had enjoyed flings with were removed or at least stopped from working with him alone.

Unlike him, Kate seemed to have little enthusiasm to work; she used her femininity to get what she wanted. I could never get away with what she did, but I was settling into the effects of my plain looks.

I'd often speak up and give ideas in meetings, if I could get a word in, resulting in me being ignored. Later, Chris would suggest the same idea and it would be taken on board. He'd be slapped on the back for coming up with it. After a time, I stopped contributing. Why bother?

Chris was considered for specialist training; they didn't ask me—I wasn't even invited to the meeting about it. Chris's specialist trainer visited to give us a talk and said it was good to see all four of us at the meeting. I counted to make sure: the boss, Chris, Kate, Tom and me.

'Five,' I suggested with a smile. He argued four, pointing at everyone but me. I'm not sure if he thought me the manager, the minute-taker or the cleaner, but I wasn't counted in his reckoning. No one corrected him, so I gave up. The staff were no better. A client asked one of the secretaries if she was in charge when she brought him in to me.

'Us girls don't know anything about that clever stuff,' she said chirpily.

'This one does,' I had to correct her with a snippy comment and a glare.

Women tend to consider each other as competition. They tend not help each other, like the men do, because they, as a rule, have no real positions of power. The men generally ignore the women, unless they are sleeping together or they at least find them attractive. This was how it was for Kate; she had the advantage over me there. Sexism isn't always a negative for the girl; sometimes it works out.

The boys pointed to a picture of Kate on the website. 'What a fantastic advert for the business,' the boss said. She had more chance of being objectified than me, but Kate was treated like a queen ... until she took things too far. But I had bigger things to worry about at home.

SANDRA'S first words to me on Messenger were, 'You are not good enough for him.'

Paddy never even admitted Sandra existed, as far as his romantic life went. He'd been alone for years, he had said. Sandra was a former beauty queen who had become a fat drunk after her husband left her for a younger model. She told me Paddy had always had a crush on her at school, but she hadn't noticed him then. He asked her out when they were older, once Monica ran off, and her head was turned, but she was never enough for him to show off about.

I was promoted to one of the girlfriends he would admit to. I was a bit overweight. I'd said I didn't care about it, so he didn't use being overweight as a trigger for me. Sandra hated being overweight; the woman her husband had left her for was slim. So that is what Paddy used against her. She told me he didn't speak to her for a month after dropping off an exercise bike to her. 'Come back and see me when you've lost a stone,' he told her.

She told me they'd gone out for five years after Monica left. Her message was a rambling, wine-assisted rant about how bad he was to her, which then developed into how much she still loved him, and then how first-rate he was in bed.

'Who the hell is Sandra?' I'd confronted him.

'Sandra? No one ... A lassie I know.' He shrugged.

'You never mentioned her.'

'Why would I?'

'You went out with her?'

'Aye, I knew her for years. I wouldn't say 'went out with.' Just a couple of months.'

'Five years?' I questioned.

'No. What you need to understand is that Sandra is crazy.'

She does act crazy. She messages me at 9pm every night with follow-up rants and abuse.

'How are you still friends with her on Facebook?' I questioned another time.

'She's harmless.' My line of questioning did not perturb him. He actually seemed to enjoy it.

'She isn't harmless. She is sending me messages—how I'm fatter and uglier than her and she can't understand what you see in me.'

'Just ignore her. She wants me back. I told you, I'm irresistible.' He laughed.

'Why are you friends with her? Do you still chat with her on Messenger?' I continued.

'No, just now and then.'

'Well, next time you are "now and then" chatting, can you tell her to stop messaging me and being horrible?'

Why was she lying? Was she lying? He got angry with me for going on about it. He couldn't see how it was a big deal. I kept going on about it until he walked out. I maybe overreacted. I didn't hear from him in a week.

I bumped into Denise in the shops. She asked how I was, and when I said I hadn't heard from Paddy, without any prompting, she replied, 'There is nothing going on with him and Sandra.' It was clear he had filled her in on his version.

'I get that, but he said he never went out with her at all.'

'He did for about a couple of months, but not now.' His version clearly included that I thought there was something going on currently, and that I was paranoid and jealous.

'Sandra's mad—she's a pisshead.' This was rich coming from Denise, whose shopping basket contained two bottles of vodka, a pack of beer, and no food items.

Paddy appeared a week later

'I've had a think, and okay, we can get back together,' he announced.

'I never asked if we could,' I dared.

'You know that is what's going to happen. It's what we do, and I'm okay with that. Paddy can be very forgiving at times. You just need to get control of that temper of yours,' he instructed.

'Okay.' I tried to keep my words to Paddy to a minimum sometimes, to save misinterpretation.

'And behave yourself, all right?'

I nodded

'I tell you, you are lucky I am here. There's not many would put up with you,' he said as he settled back into the armchair.

There was no apology for the silent treatment or for lying about a five-year relationship.

AT WORK, Kate had been pushing her luck for a while. The positive workplace sexism that benefitted her only could go so far. Several times she left before everyone else or decided to have a last-minute day off, and then the staff would see her out shopping or doing the garden.

She wouldn't work her fair share of public holidays. She even took a day off when I was on holiday and not there to cover for her. The manager told Bossman, and when he asked if she had done this before, it came out that she did this often. Bossman often flew off the handle and yelled. His vernacular was littered with swear words, so it was unsurprising she got a verbal bashing and he called her a 'fucking lazy bitch.'

She couldn't understand his attitude. How dare he? You couldn't blame her for being perplexed; no one had ever spoken like that to her before. If she changed her mind about working at the last minute and wanted a day off, she expected people to work around it. What mattered to her was that she was happy, never mind anyone else.

Tom continued to work with us, but Kate never returned. Soon, Tom announced that they were leaving together for a year working abroad. They were engaged by then. I heard Kate was devastated by Bossman's words, and Tom was angry at the way she had been treated. Tom always backed her up, no matter what.

Paddy never ever backed me up. Instead the smallest thing would set him against me. Any dispute I had he would take the other's side.

I let out a flat in town to a tenant, who was always very demanding. She sent me a text message in the middle of the night to complain the catch on the door didn't work, so she slammed it, which caused the handle to break and she hurt her hand. The text was littered with swear words and a threat to report me to some authority.

Annoyed, I said in front of Paddy, 'Flippin' middle of the night. Breaks the door then blames me. How's that my fault? I'm fed up with her, really. The bloody cheek! I've a mind to go over there right now and chuck her out.'

'My God, the way you treat people is disgusting!' Paddy shook his head.

His reaction to things always surprised me. He always had a different angle. My reaction to the text was the problem.

'What?' I felt broadsided. 'I've not done anything. I am pissed off at this idiot.' I half-laughed, hoping he would see the funny side.

'You were going around to attack that poor woman, drag her out onto the street, and then God knows what. She has a right to complain.'

'At three in the morning? I said I *felt* like going round there and chucking her out. I'm not doing it. I never even ...' I could see this was going wrong.

'That's what you are like, though, and I have to say ...' he paused. Was that a smile? 'Monica would have never have behaved like this.'

'Your wife who cheated on you and left you behaves better than me?' I dared.

'Oh my God. How could you bring that up?' He had forgotten he had mentioned her first, despite it being mere seconds ago. 'To hell with this.' He walked again and didn't answer the phone for days.

I thought he'd calm down. We were due to go to an event the following week, so I waited for him with my coat on until it got dark. I messaged, and he didn't answer for two weeks. After I gave up, he turned up.

'What happened?' I asked.

'I didn't feel like coming out after your performance the week before.'

'Why didn't you call? We are adults—you could at least tell me.'

'When you start behaving like an adult, I'll start treating you like one. I needed some time alone after what you said about Monica.'

I couldn't understand how this was about her. 'You could have said you needed some time on your own.'

'You need to realise I am not here for you to boss around, Angela. I thought you wanted to be calmer. I gave you time to calm down and now you can learn to make a decision to improve on that.'

'I don't understand any of this. The tenant apologised to me, by the way. She'd been drinking and had an argument with her boyfriend ... but maybe I need to calm down.'

'And maybe I should have called. But it's worth it now, to see you fretting like this. Shows you love me.' He looked satisfied.

I was confused. Was it a test? He knew I'd feel guilty about overreacting and wish I had been sweeter. It meant he could practically get away with anything.

To prove I loved him, I had to become a nicer person. It would also allow him to do whatever he wanted and make me feel guilty for complaining. And if he wanted a break to get up to whatever he wanted, he just needed to provoke my anger, wait for me to lose my temper, then walk out blaming me.

It seemed I had been sucked back into another circle of stress and drama. Paddy had me on a string, but at least work was keeping me steady. I never could have predicted how that was all about to unravel.

FORTY-SIX

You can catch a thief, but you cannot catch a liar. Sociopaths have little conscience and do not care about hurting others to get what they want. I didn't know it when they left, but this was how Kate and Tom planned their revenge.

Chris had suffered some sort of breakdown. He was seen drugged in public, and there were rumours of sexual harassment of a staff member.

Workplace sexism is a strange thing. Chris and Bossman used to objectify women right in front of me, as if I were another piece of furniture in the coffee room. I would listen to them, thinking, How do I respond to this? I shouldn't overreact.

'I read that a famous lad's magazine has shown a transgender model,' I once said, hoping we could move onto a topic about gender but still on the theme of pin-ups. The boss hadn't heard about it, but Chris had and described her in anatomical detail. This led him to chat *about his Thailand experiences. Chris had many tales of Thai massage parlours and strip joints.*

After the incident with the staff member, he was removed with immediate effect to work in the Edinburgh office. It was like a church cover-up. No police were involved; he was simply moved to another parish.

I HEARD from Bossman that Tom and Kate were returning from abroad to take over from Chris. I was relieved. I was carrying a lot of the work myself, and I needed help and a chance to take annual leave.

Bossman told me they had plans to open a new business together, similar to what we were doing, but a new branch, brand, and premises. It was all hush-hush.

I'd been overlooked again.

He went on with enthusiasm, telling me they had held talks with the local council and were set to receive a major council contract. Building permissions and regulations needed looking at too. He couldn't wait to show me the plans on his next visit. Initially, Tom was to come and work with us until it all was all finalised and signed off.

On the day Tom was due start work, I got a call from a stressed sounding Sophie, our manager, to come and cover for Tom, who hadn't turned up. It reminded me of Kate's behaviour from before. I went in and was filled in on the details later. At a short break, I found Sophie red-faced. She had been crying. She blurted out that she had called Tom when he was late, and he had raged at her. What she reported seemed out of character.

'How dare you call me and tell me off? I'm not just a member of the staff, and I have my reasons—I'm definitely not coming in now. I'll never be there!' said mild-mannered Tom. Sophie called the boss, who turned on her, swearing and shouting as usual.

THE BUCKET LIST   201

'What the hell did you say to him?' he demanded. She protested her innocence, that she had merely asked him if he slept in or if his car had broken down. There were more swear words, and she ended up in the state I saw her.

I carried on working, but I couldn't help being curious about the drama going on. By the end of the day, it was clear things had not been resolved. I was instructed to come in again.

The following day, after work, I got a call from Bossman asking if I had heard from Tom. I explained I didn't communicate with them outside of work. I feigned no knowledge of the manager's story.

'Why? What is wrong? Is he ill?'

'No, he says he's not coming to work for us now. It's all Sophie's fault. He says she was rude to him on the phone, and he couldn't put up with that.'

Bossman did not sound convinced. It seemed an over-the-top reaction, and that was from me, the woman who was apparently always overreacting. He said not to worry as he thought Tom might calm down and come to work as planned next week. Bossman was bound to sort it all out; he was charming, when he wasn't swearing and shouting. They were business partners, after all, with a huge council contract in the pipeline. It was a spat and things would blow over.

But that's not what happened at all. What happened next surprised everyone.

FORTY-SEVEN

" I was walking home from a rare night out when I was attacked. They knew my name and said I was 'a fake' before hitting me in the head. I'd been drinking, and it was dark, so I didn't get any description enough for the police, just the vague shape of an attacker wearing all black.

I decided I hated everyone and blocked anyone I didn't trust, which was most people from the area, off my social media.

Paddy arrived after I texted him. I thought he'd look after me. His face was hard, his eyes narrowed, and his brow low. His lips were drawn tight, a single line of redness. He was furious—not with my attacker, but with me.

My huffy Facebook blocking of people was built into the worst crime since the Holocaust. It was never forgotten, brought up in all future arguments. It got the best reaction from me because it was so ridiculous. From *then on, this episode was referred to as, 'that time you abused my friends.'*

Not once did Paddy ask how the cut on my eye was healing or whether I was emotionally okay.

'HOW COULD YOU? Some of those people you blocked are my friends! What will I say to them? I can't believe the way you abuse people.'

'I didn't abuse them, though, Paddy. Please! I blocked them because I don't know who attacked me. I was upset. They must have been local.' I wanted to talk about the attack, which I thought was the point. 'My attacker knew my name! I was scared someone was looking at my stuff, getting angry enough to attack me over it. It's only Facebook!'

'You would have abused them, though, given the chance.'

I was being told off for something I *might* have done, all to stoke the insecurity that even I didn't know what I was capable of. He wasn't interested in anything anyone had done to me. He continued with a lengthy monologue, the longest ever, shouting until I was curled in a ball on the kitchen floor. I was crying, whimpering. I couldn't win, even after being attacked on the street.

'Please stop, please. Leave me alone. Please.'

'Look at you—pathetic. Who does that? Have some respect.' The door slammed, and he was gone.

Later, he used my reaction to gauge whether he'd done well enough with his abuse. I learnt that to get him to stop, I'd need to get to the crying, curled-up stage.

Paddy came back after a couple of weeks, but not to apologise. His explanation for not being around was that I'd told him to leave me alone, so he did. He said that he'd decided we needed to be together, but I needed to get my act together.

I didn't get off scot-free after he came back. I didn't get to go to the next friends' party as a punishment.

'You can't just come back after that and hang out with my friends, not after what you did. You hurt a lot of people. I can let it go, but I can't speak for them.'

I stayed at home and painted my back room. On the night of the party, I messaged Denise apologising for blocking her on Facebook. She said she had no idea about my attack and hadn't noticed she'd been blocked. Within half an hour, all the monkeys added me as a friend.

Later that year, Paddy and I visited my sister's house for a family party. I didn't feel well, so I went to lie down. On my way home with him, I saw a newspaper report about a TV star who died of a burst appendix.

'That was exactly how I was feeling,' I told him. 'I was suffering those same symptoms she had at the beginning.'

He laughed and said, 'Of course. At the very least, you'd have an illness that would make headlines.'

It got worse, and I ended up at the hospital, where, indeed, appendicitis was diagnosed. My mum called him to tell him they were going to operate. She was shocked at his short reply. 'Let me know when she gets out.'

I was operated on that night. I was fine to go in a couple of days, but I was still in pain from the operation when my sister called to check I was better and to ask if Paddy had been around to help. I told her he hadn't called.

She told me that when I'd gone upstairs to lie down at her party, he had said, 'You see what I have to deal with? She's always doing things like this.'

'Don't know what you mean. I think she isn't well,' my sister had replied. He had tried to put it in her head that I was being difficult, and he was a saint to put up with me. She was surprised and angry at his callous indifference for my well-being.

I gave up my version of the silent treatment and called to tell him

I was upset he never seemed to care. There was no pause when I told of the hurt he caused me, no pause to suggest a pricked conscience. An apology might normally come in that situation, or even an explanation, or an excuse. I got none of those. The rebuke I gave him made him angry, and he abused me twice as hard. Then the work scenario exploded.

THE LOCAL RADIO NEWS, presented by minor celebrity Michael James, announced a new business would be opening in town, run by Kate and Tom. I was confused. Bossman did not get a mention, and I hadn't heard it would be so soon. But then, they often missed me out with big news. Had they made up? It had been two weeks to the day since Tom had not shown up for work, and he hadn't been in since.

I arrived at work to find all the staff gathered for a meeting. Sophie explained that Kate and Tom had taken the council contract for themselves alone, and they were opening up without Bossman. I asked if they had simply dropped Bossman from the new business and council plans. No, they'd arranged different premises altogether, a separate logo and website all while pretending to take the contract with the boss.

Sophie expanded that the belief was they had been planning this all along. Bossman had bought a new office for the purpose of being leased to the new business. Now he was left with an empty building. I questioned what the people at the council were doing, as they must have gone to double meetings, one with them all together and another with just Kate and Tom. There was no answer.

I carried on working, but I couldn't get it out of my mind. At home, I scoured the internet, looking for clues. I rigorously checked the council planning permission site. Planning applications for the building were under Kate's name, dated from three months ago. At the same time, Bossman was applying for them for *his* new building.

It had all been happening in a council office I could see from my window the whole time.

I hadn't had a panic attack since Eric, but the manipulation, the deviousness on such an incredible scale brought my anxiety on again. I Googled some more and found their names on a business website in England from a year ago. They hadn't been abroad at all, although their blurb said they had. They lied about that too.

'Why?' I asked Bossman.

'She hates me. I swore at her on the phone.'

'You swear at everyone on the phone.'

He managed a little smile.

'Is that all? Is that it?'

There seemed to be no other reason for it. That slight against Kate was enough to escalate their whole revenge plot. It explained Tom's bizarre fake offence when Sophie called him.

I wondered when I would ever be free of sociopathic liars. Again, I felt stupid and helpless. It wasn't directed at me, at least, until I became a pawn in their wars.

I was associated with Bossman, and I had been the one who didn't cover for her that one time, so I got caught in the crossfire. Every client we worked with came to us complaining. Occasionally, complaints would happen, but this time, every single one of our clients had been contacted by them for a free assessment of our work. All had been instructed to get refunds so Tom and Kate could redo their work 'properly'. A few said it had been suggested they sue us to get the money for the improvements Kate and Tom would make. One by one, the clients dwindled away. I eventually left work, citing a lack of work and an excess of stress.

I started looking for a new job, something different. I still earned money from gigs to tide me over. After one gig, I walked by the place I had been attacked. I stopped, closed my eyes, and flashed back to that night. I leaned against the wall and tried to remember. The female voice came first, then the slim frame and a glimpse of wispy white-blonde hair. Kate? Did she blame me for being associated with

Bossman? Or was I an easy way to hurt him?

I wished I were back on the island. I would have preferred a glass over the head in a bar. I would have taken it all now. Why was everything falling apart?

'They're simply building their business.' People would defend them. But was it necessary to damage others to get ahead? They were steely like Brenda; liars like Eric.

PADDY CONTINUED his love-hate relationship with me. He started helping out a local woman whose husband had died young from leukaemia. He was resoundingly seen as a great guy for helping organise her removals and painting her hallway. He let everyone know. He organised a fundraiser for her and made the papers.

I was annoyed. I had been left alone to paint my own back room while he went to a party.

'She is on her own,' he explained.

'So am I,' I answered. But I was being petty. As a young widow, she was more deserving of help than I was. You get plaudits for helping the widowed woman whose husband died tragically young. No one cares if you help your girlfriend—that's taken for granted.

We carried on the pattern and went away for a break to Kenmore. Callum was young, skipping ahead and walking along a wall.

'Can you not keep him under control?' Paddy grumbled.

'He's all right.' I shrugged. I didn't react enough.

He needed to go in harder. 'My kids would never act like that.' I should have known his aim was to rile me, but I didn't care this time.

'Your kids are scared to do anything. You compare me to Monica, and you compare my child to yours. Nothing I do is ever good enough.' I stormed.

Of course, I was wrong for this. When we returned to the lodge, after the silent walk back, he locked himself in the room and wouldn't let me in.

After I put Callum to bed, I thought of killing myself. I looked out over the loch. I could walk in there and never be seen again.

Instead, I drank half a bottle of whiskey, resorted to my favourite self-harm mode, and slept on the couch. I thought there was no way out of this cycle.

The following day, I had a blinding headache from the drink and the physical abuse. Paddy made me promise to get a hold of my temper and to never speak of his children the way I had the day before.

'Callum deserves a better mother than you're being,' he snapped.

I agreed. Worn out, I believed it too.

Once home, I picked up my iPad to check Facebook. I didn't usually use it for that, as I preferred the laptop, but the iPad was by my bed, and the laptop was downstairs. A message popped up.

Gillian.

I didn't recognise the name. The message made no sense.

I scrolled back until I realised it wasn't from my Facebook at all but from Paddy's. He had borrowed my iPad while we were away. The night he'd locked himself in the room, he had signed onto Facebook and left himself logged in.

I froze, but curiosity got the better of me. He had been chatting with Gillian about her husband and the time she and Paddy had spent together; how blissful it was. It became clear the time they spent together was without Gillian's husband. My heart was pounding and my mouth was dry.

I put the device down and got a drink of water from the kitchen downstairs. *I should log out,* I thought. *It's private.* But I ran back up and picked it up again.

They went on. I was never mentioned once. I checked her profile. She was a tiny woman with short-cropped grey hair and glasses. She lived with several dogs and a husband with a ruddy face. Then, a message from Sandra popped onto the screen. I jumped.

I scrolled back through her messages. It was enlightening. Paddy had told me he rarely spoke to her; however, there were hundreds of messages, all recent, and they had chatted for hours. They talked about what a wonderful time they had together, flirted, and occasionally, she would beg him to take her back. Sometimes, she would even ask him about me. In those cases, Paddy would either change the subject or deny anything serious was going on, saying I was 'something and nothing.'

He was also managing to speak to both of them at once. I checked more messages. They were all from women: some single, some married. I even saw some flirty messages to the widow he had helped, but she reminded him he had a girlfriend and her husband had just died. I loved her at that moment.

A couple of the women picked on me for being fat. One thought my tits were too big. Another thought I dressed sluttily. They were insulting, but at least they acknowledged I existed.

Messages from Linda, Mandy, and Denise in a group chat talked about how mad I was and mentioned how crazy Sandra was. The local glamour-puss got trashed. They were laughing at us all.

'She's obviously mad,' they said about me. 'I don't know how she keeps a job down.' They all agreed I was off my head. For someone who didn't believe in mental illness, Paddy was quick to diagnose insanity.

'I can't help it if all these women find me irresistible!!!' He wrote. The monkeys all laughed with differing emojis. I focused back in on the Gillian conversation until it became sexual. I felt sick. How was this happening? Who the hell was Gillian?

I logged off once they were both satisfied and called it a night. I messaged Paddy that I had seen all his conversations, downed a huge brandy, and left a comment on Gillian's photo with one of her dogs, 'Bitch!'

He arrived at my door within an hour. I didn't answer.

FORTY-EIGHT

After three consecutive days of Paddy trying to speak to me, I eventually let him in. We spoke in my kitchen. He admitted that Gillian was an old friend who was lonely and came up for a cup of tea, and one thing led to another.

I suggested that a cup of tea should not lead to anything other than a bloody biscuit when it's with someone else's grey-haired wife. Then I threw him out.

Of course, he then needed to initiate damage control. Everyone had to know I was insane. He told them all I made up an affair with him and Gillian and that was why I wrote the comment. It was a brave move, in case mud stuck, but it worked.

He deleted all the conversations and changed his passwords. Back then, I lacked the wit and the know-how to screenshot. I'd be all over that now.

He maintained I had breached his trust and defamed poor Gillian by telling everyone they were having an affair. He assumed I'd told all and acted like I *already had, when the only person I had spoken to about it was him.*

Soon, the police paid me a visit. He and Linda had convinced them that, somehow, I'd broken the law. Paddy had charmed the policewoman, and they had character assassinated me to the point that even she thought I was a crazy woman.

Linda, of course, seemed credible to them, as she believed everything Paddy said. They took my iPad and laptop and checked them in front of me for what I'd been writing to people.

The police left, giving me no warnings or charges. Even they looked like they had been duped and it had just dawned on them. At the time, I wondered whether Paddy had the power to hypnotise people.

A month later, I was heading back to the Kenmore Lodge, now with my mother instead of him. While I was waiting at the bus station, he texted me to ask for forgiveness. He said Linda had been the one who had contacted the police. I partly believed that. Linda had clearly been given the line that I was a maniac spreading lies, and who knew what I could do next. Once she called the police, he had to go along with it.

He knew I hadn't done anything wrong. He'd gone too far this time. It was the first time he said sorry, although he did seem a little peeved he missed out on his holiday. 'Yes, I will forgive you,' I texted as I sat on the bus. 'But I don't want you back.'

'You are amazing,' was the answer. It was not a compliment. It was amazing for him to be able to act like a piece of shit and get away with it. I was the perfect girlfriend for him.

MY INCOME TOOK a hit with me leaving the business, as I hadn't yet found another job. I loved the area and my beautiful house, so I ran for local council when the chance arose. The local man, Douglas, was seeking re-election.

We attended a husting which Michael James, the radio host, chaired. One of the voters asked a question about a well-known council scandal he was wrapped up in. Douglas had been in charge of that department in the council, but he denied any wrongdoing. He went so far as to lie and tell a different story to the one he had at the enquiry. It was all broadcast live on the local radio station. I cringed, ready for the fall out.

Michael said nothing. He didn't follow it up at all. I was left stunned; Michael fancied himself as a journalist, but he'd missed his chance.

'Did you hear him?' I asked my friend after it. 'He was lying?'

She said she did hear. Everyone did. I thought I stood a chance, as that alone should have scuppered him, but he still won with a resounding majority. Another liar had beaten me, and I had to think again.

The band was still going, at least. We had a regular gig at the local social club. I went in one day and suddenly they said I couldn't keep my equipment there anymore. There was no explanation as to why; the reason was 'the committee had decided.' It made it difficult for me because I now had to transport everything there and back every week, but I soldiered on.

I couldn't understand the frosty attitude when another time I asked for change for the car park. Then I saw the photos of the new board of committee members on the wall. Kate's face smiled down at me as Social Convener. Soon, the bar staff informed me they didn't need my services at all; the committee had decided they did not want a band.

Within a month, a new band started. I saw the poster on the noticeboard the same day I saw Kate for the last time, through the café window. I passed by and they were all there together: Michael the radio host, Douglas the councillor, and Kate—all having lunch. None of them looked embarrassed when they saw me.

I asked around and found out that Douglas was Kate's uncle and Michael a distant relative. Of course, that explained the secret council meetings, and the lack of journalistic vigour.

WHILE I SEARCHED for alternative employment, I decided to date again. I did it to stop thinking about Paddy and to prove I could move on. I went on two dates with Ewen: one to a concert and another to the theatre. I hadn't heard from Paddy in months.

Mandy, flying monkey two, sat behind us in the theatre. We nodded our 'hellos', and I sank into my seat. The following day, Paddy messaged. He couldn't live without me and we should try again. I decided three years was too much to throw away.

He promised we could live together and forget everything from the past. Instead, we went back into our usual pattern of blame-game sessions until the last time, when he did not return. I'd been replaced.

Barbara appeared, as if from nowhere, commenting on all his posts on Facebook—liking and loving everything. She was from Liver-pool. He had run out of local supply, so he needed to spread the net wider. He knew her from years ago.

Soon, she gathered a bunch of new Facebook pals—all the monkeys joined in liking her posts and sucking her into the gang. She was not glamorous but quite plain. Perhaps, like Gillian and Sandra, she had been pretty in the past. They had all lost their glamour, but Paddy could still gather together enough enthusiasm for them. However, they needed some improvement, and that was his special-ity. The fact she was married was not an issue. Perhaps it was even a benefit.

Then another person appeared on Facebook, also called Barbara but with a different surname. This one had no picture and no friends at all. It was 'Barbara Number One' incognito. I could tell it was her, as she wrote every comment with a 'lol' as punctuation.

I commented on a post of his, which she took the wrong way. She wrote me a long-winded message rebuking me for bullying him. It was all about how I treated him, how I couldn't accept his atheism, how I was a Bible-basher and a bad example of a believer in God. There were several exclamation marks and misspellings in there, and I recognised it as an angry message, probably fuelled by alcohol. It confirmed my suspicion that she was the next romantic entanglement.

She messaged from a fake account so she could chat to him away from her husband's eye. She did not have the moral high ground. He must have ripped my personality to shreds while chatting to her. I told her I knew she was 'Barbara Number One' and married, and then I blocked her.

FORTY-NINE

"Paddy and I had no official break-up, as such. I found out we were finished when Sandra messaged me that she heard we split. She veered from bad story to worse of how he treated her. Then she moved on to how I was never up to his standards. She had been a beauty queen in her youth, at least. She still loved him and would get him back if she could lose some weight.

'Bugger off, Sandra,' I wrote, and blocked her.

Barbara made me remember that I was once the woman Paddy loved to make feel insecure about his ex. I was the woman Paddy set against Monica in a weird competition I never signed up to. I was the woman who was told Monica was the worst person in the world, and yet ...

It was strange that he spoke of how he hated his ex-wife and what she had done to him, but he also made me feel that I could never measure up to her.

I don't know if anything he said about Monica was true, based on the lies he told Barbara about me. He had *created a new bizarre triangle with himself, Barbara, and me, instead of himself, Monica, and me.*

I secretly thanked Barbara for showing me how I was from a distance, for sacrificing herself so I could escape.

Again, I packed up, sold up, and moved—this time back home to East Lothian.

I stopped running away after that. It took me a long time to feel even a little bit better.

I'm glad Paddy didn't try to get back with me then, as it could have gone on forever. But he still wasted my precious time.

Fourth Section—Perthshire 1

- Kate
- Tom
- Chris
- Michael—radio station
- Douglas—council

Club, building, attics

enjoy
every
moment.

FIFTY

"It's late October, orange Halloween decorations in the shops match the trees outside. I've been cooped up for a long time, writing all those memories and ideas. I need to get out.

I've tried to stay in, tried to fight the urges, but I need to go back to Perthshire. I have a few scores to settle there, and I have waited for what seems like forever.

The thing about serial killing is the police look for a connection. They would struggle to connect any of these tragic passings or even to find a connection between these people. They are all different. None of them knew each other.

How are they related? By me. But then, I met Miss Moleman, Mark, and Eric all years apart. How they die is different too.

An old lady dies in her sleep.

A middle-aged man falls down stairs.

A guy drives off a cliff.

And ... however I deal with the next two. They are

both in Perthshire, so there is a connection there, but I don't think they ever met.

I searched Google recently and found out Chris was already dead. He died of a heart attack in a brothel in Thailand. At least he died happy, but the article I read mentioned it cost his family a fortune to get him flown home.

I also Googled Kate and Tom, who appear to be thriving, on the surface. They've moved to a huge home, opened another branch. They're still monopolising the area, regarding business. Another council contract has helped them out, but they were not settled at that.

Money seems like no object, superficially, but wealth often comes with financial struggles underneath. It looks like they're spending more than they're earning and are close to bankruptcy with their revenge strategy. They are at it again: renovating an old building near the centre of town for new bigger and more impressive premises.

How on Earth did they get planning permission passed for that listed building? That's right, her uncle Douglas on the council is sorting that out for her!

Douglas seems like he is Teflon-coated. Google revealed he was caught drunk-driving, seven times over the limit after drinking at the club all night, and he had his license taken off him. The arrogance of the man—to think he wouldn't get caught! And the gall to stay on the council after his reputation took a battering. I have never been that bold.

AS SOON AS I enter Preston's flat, his dog, Boaby, barks, and his cat, Willie, who always comes to the door to inspect who is coming in, looks me up and down and walks away. Preston thinks he has funny names for his pets.

'Don't touch my Willie now,' he says. Or he shouts, 'Boaby, Boaby' down the park and gets away with it.

A corner of Preston's living room is set out like a small office. It has a tan-brown leather swivel chair and a desk. Someone is leaning forward, writing on the desk. He sits upright, so his red head appears.

'Hi there.' He swings around when he hears me enter.

I can barely muster up the strength to be civil to this smiling monster who is trying to be friendly. He is not dead behind the eyes. There so much going on there. I feel like he looks inside me.

Preston's brother wears a tan-brown leather jacket that matches the chair, so it looks like his head possesses no body. Close-up, wisps of grey pepper his temple and sprout from his nose and ears.

He has surprised me, and anxiety grips my throat. He stands up, a towering, broad-shouldered presence.

'You must be Angela. How are you today?'

I manage a nod.

'Preston never told me how attractive you are?'

Is he flirting with me? I feel sick knowing what he has done.

'Ugh-huh,' I mumble. An awkward silence ensues. I can't muster up any small talk. Preston appears after a flush from the toilet.

'Hiya,' he says chirpily. Then, stony-faced, 'Mother is dead.'

Red has come to tell him.

'Sorry to hear that,' I practically whisper. Red is smiling, or I should say, leering, rather a lot for a grieving son.

I pull my cardigan up over my bosom to protect it from his glare.

'You can still talk. You may continue,' Preston says formally as he sits on the edge of the sofa. I am directed to take a seat too.

Preston's face is solemn, and I am aware there is official business happening. Red talks on and on about his mother's flat and what they will spend the money on once it sells for a pretty penny. It is a matter of hours since her passing in the night, but he has moved onto the positive side of the money left and the practical details.

'Uh-huh,' replies Preston several times. It is all he can say.

As he leaves, Red kisses Preston on the cheek, and then he comes towards me.

What is he doing? I smell the smoke from his cigarettes. He leans in to kiss me goodbye on the cheek, and I feel a surge of nausea.

Preston smiles unconvincingly. *Can Red not see the tension in this situation?* I think he knows and does not care, or maybe he even likes it.

The door closes. We can breathe again.

'Are you okay?' I assume Preston's quietness is because he is shocked, upset at his mother's passing.

'Oh, thank fuck for that. I could hardly keep that going much longer.' He laughs and laughs. I expect him to start crying, but he is doubled-over instead.

'One down, one to go!'

'Hell, Preston, she's your mother,' I scold him.

'Not all mothers are equal,' he bites. 'Crème brûlée.'

I apologise that I won't make the funeral. I am going away for a couple of weeks break in the campervan. Luckily, John hates sleeping in the van, so it's taken for granted he won't come. Preston says he doesn't know if he'll end up going to the funeral himself. He instructs me to talk about something else.

'Okay ... What are you doing today?' I venture.

'Going to the vet with my Willie.'

'Is it Dr. Gorgeous, the vet? The one in North Street? Oh, I like him. Jen and Jill at work were always on about him.'

'Eh, yes. But, lady, I believe you and your work pals are barking up the wrong tree there ...'

'How do you mean?'

He is winking at me, looking smug.

'Oh. Really?'

'Oh yes. You are not just barking up the wrong tree. You are in the whole wrong bloody forest, doll.'

I laugh loudly at this. I wondered why the vet was single.

'Hilarious—you like him?' I ask.

'Oh yeah. Be still, my beating soul.'

'Oh, Preston, your soul? Not your heart? How does your soul beat?' I shake my head.

'Mine does.'

'Only you, mate. What's wrong with the cat?' I look around for Willie, who could pounce from anywhere.

'Usual jabs for my Willie.'

I snigger at this, as required. 'And what is your chat-up line? Do you like my Willie?' I suggest.

'Nice. If you like my Willie, wait till you see my Boaby.'

'Would you like to stroke my Willie?' We giggle like silly children.

'Where are you going in the van?' he asks.

'Going to Perthshire to walk alpacas.'

'I'm not asking any more about that.'

'It's on my bucket list.'

'No fucking idea what that's all about, but you enjoy yourself, hen. You used to live up that way, didn't you?

'Yes, in the Isles, then there.' I give no more information.

Back home, I get packing. In the middle of it, I wonder why the landline is ringing. Who could be calling?

Is it the hospital? It can't be the hospital today.

Is it the police? I've always been anxious in front of the police, even though I've never done anything unlawful until now.

It's a scammer, something about an accident. I fling the receiver down on them.

Perthshire, I'm on my way.

FIFTY-ONE

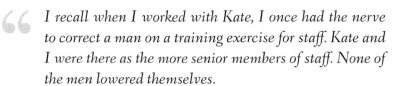

" I recall when I worked with Kate, I once had the nerve to correct a man on a training exercise for staff. Kate and I were there as the more senior members of staff. None of the men lowered themselves.

Neither Kate nor any of the girls backed me up when he refused my correction and argued back. I had to concede.

Afterwards, they agreed I was right, but they all wanted to get away early so had let the man win the argument. They suggested I lighten up.

'Hey, the man was only doing his job,' they said. Badly, I thought. That's as brave as I ever got. I was never bold enough to tough things out. I always left, got away. I even had to leave my amazing house for them.

After I moved away, the Perthshire mob haunted me for quite a while. I think it was three years to get rid of all the consequences of their actions.

I blocked them on social media until recently. They

were the hovering types, snoopers who gave nothing away. All of my victims seem like this, don't they? They have so much to hide. I am an open book in contrast. Well ... I was.

I'm secretive this year, but I'm writing it all down for posterity.

I'll give them closure one day. They'll know why it happened. I'll put a full stop on the thoughts and prayers for them.

I PARK the van in the local campsite and pull on my boots. I feel older than I am as I struggle to get them on without sweating and grunting. When stepping out of the van, I make a noise with the effort.

I take a walk down to the town. Tom and Kate's new premises, currently with a skip outside, sit right between the radio station and the social club. They are all on the same block in a side street off the High Street. There is a car park in front and to the side of the club, and then a block of flats. A derelict cash and carry warehouse takes up the other side of the road.

It's easy to get into the club. Social clubs in rural locations aren't covered with CCTV and complex systems of security. It's like going back in time. They are public buildings and have limited funds, mostly just about keeping afloat; therefore, there's nothing to steal and nothing needing protection. They aren't expecting to get broken into.

This club has a camera at the door. You press the buzzer, and they can see who it is and let you in via a switch at the bar. That way, there is no need to leave the till to let you in, and they don't need to pay a doorman.

I still possess the fob I owned from years ago. I check whether it still works—it does, but I still use the buzzer system today. I know they don't look to see who it is half the time. I've been at the bar, and they would let people in by reaching around to the cupboard for the switch while still chatting to the punters. I once asked about the camera. It doesn't record and save footage; that type was too expensive.

I order a drink at the bar. I don't recognise the barman. It's not Fergus. I stare at the partition between the bar and the main hall. At times, it would be pulled back to open the bar and hall into one for bigger functions.

The partition was closed on that early Sunday morning when I cleared away my things from the hall for the last time. I had sung at a charity event the night before. Fergus, the barman, hadn't seen me come in. He had gone to get stock, so I'd let myself in with my fob. I quietly set about piling all my equipment up at the door of the hall and was putting the cables in the storage box when I heard voices through the partition. I stopped dead still when I heard a familiar voice.

'Not bad, not bad at all!' Kate sounded happy.

I stood as still as I could and edged closer to the gap in the partition. I tried to not even breathe.

'Last night went well. How much was brought in?' asked Fergus.

'A fair amount, shall we say. Thousands. I was up late counting it all,' Kate enthused. I could almost see her rubbing her hands together.

'Excellent! You know, I put in a fair bit of extra work with the decorating and clearing up, and you said ...' ventured Fergus.

'I've factored that in. I'll bung some up to them upstairs. Then I'll see you right. Don't you worry, you've helped me out a lot, and you know the saying, "you scratch my back ..."' They laughed.

'Great, and how about yourself?'

'Let's just say, between you and me, there will be 3,000 pounds for the charity ... once Tom and I get a decent holiday out of it.'

'Too right,' agreed Fergus.

I SIGH AUDIBLY, back in the present, and the barman looks over. I smile. I mention I'm going to the toilet and ask him to look after my jacket. He glances around—there is no one else in the place—and nods.

The bar and hall are one part of the building in the more modern extension. Through the massive double doors, I head past the toilets and into the older section, which has a huge main door that stays permanently locked. It was the main door in years gone by, but now everyone uses the extension door, where the bar and hall are.

I look into the downstairs room, where I used to store my equipment until I was banned. It is empty apart from a table, extra chairs, and random boxes.

I head up the grand stairs, which houses three sets of ladders, to the first-floor landing. Rooms spill off this, I imagine for the committee meetings. They were always on a Thursday night. I look up and see what I am searching for: the attic hatch. I have been gone a while.

'All right?' asks the barman on my return.

'Yeah.' But I shake my head. 'Not feeling very well. Heading back for a lie-down,' I announce before picking up my jacket and leaving.

From the warehouse wall, I watch the club for no time at all until I see the barman at the side of the hall emptying the bins. I nip in the door, using my fob, and straight to the toilets, meeting no one. I stay there awhile to catch my breath. Then, with another burst of energy, I head up the stairs to the attic, picking up a set of ladders on my way. I hope the barman has no need to come through to the older building.

The attics of the three buildings are connected. From here, I can access the soon-to-be-new premises and the radio station building. Lots of renovations have been going on in the middle building, including some in the attic. The hatch is already open, a ladder leading down from it. I peer out. It's after 5pm on a Friday, and the builders have already clocked off. I know Kate is still here because her car is outside. The one thing they did put on their social media is their fancy car.

I wait and watch Kate on the top floor of the building. I see her come out of what I assume is an office and go down the stairs. She doesn't see me creep down the ladder from the attic. I sneak into a storeroom, among lots of stationery—it's quite satisfying. The store-room is shelved all the way around, with a floor to ceiling set of dividing shelves. I crouch behind the stocked dividing shelf, which acts as a wall obscuring me from view. I crouch low, making myself small, and wait.

Eventually, Kate comes in carrying a box. I stand and, using all my strength, I tip the shelves over onto her. She screams as it all comes toppling down.

Most people don't act like footballers when they are hurt. They don't roll around moaning or complaining. Mostly they are quiet ... until they grasp what has happened and start to check what works on their body and what doesn't. Kate is still.

Then she stirs and moans. She is dazed, mumbling. I can't deal with her lolling about.

When she begins to move some of the boxes off herself, I crack her hard enough on the head with a fire extinguisher to stun her, at least.

I leave her there and go to the office, where I plant two empty whiskey bottles from my rucksack.

Wearing gloves, of course, I turn off Kate's phone and wheel her chair to the storeroom. I check her pulse. She is still living.

I make a tourniquet out of an elastic band and wrap it around her wrist, so I can inject alcohol into the vein in her hand. It might kill her, or it will at least show she has been drinking. I remove the band from her wrist and scratch her hand with some debris to hide the pinhole from detection.

After placing the toppled office chair at her feet, I head upstairs to the attic, where the builder must have left a blowtorch on. *Tut-tut. Careless. A terrible set of circumstances.*

I don't know what they will blame this on: her drinking, the stupid workplace accident of standing on a chair (with added impaired judgment due to the drink), or the builder's carelessness.

'She must have drunkenly grabbed the shelves to steady herself and became trapped under them,' they'll say. That's if they find any of those details after the fire.

There are so many flammable items on this building site that the fire burns well. From my spot above the club's main building, I can see it blaze along to the radio station attic. I stay to watch for a minute, and then I head down, replace the hatch, rehome the ladders in the stairs, and sit in the toilets.

I settle down in the cubicle. It's been a lot of effort, and I'm wound up. I try not hanging around, but I also mustn't be seen leaving.

I decide I need to get out now. Through the doors into the extension hallway, I see that no one is there. I take a chance on meeting someone coming in the front door or leaving the bar. I don't run, but I march purposefully to the hall doors, further on from the bar. Once in the hall, I know there is a fire escape to a path at the back. It leads to the side of the building and the bins.

Done with the possibility of meeting the barman again, I climb the four-foot wall to the council car park, first checking the coast is clear. It's dark enough now that I feel less exposed.

I go via the back streets after pulling on a red wig. You can never discount the curtain-twitchers. You can't legislate for the lonely. I pull up my hoodie as I enter the campsite, to hide the red, and head back to the van.

While I listen for the sirens, I change and bag my clothes and use the baby wipes in the glove box to clean myself up. I help myself to the local malt, for my nerves, and I actually start to relax.

It's a whole hour before I hear anything. There are no homes in that street facing the carnage. The windows of the flats at the side of the club car park look in another direction, so it would have taken some time to be reported.

I drink until I am unconscious and give up worrying about being caught.

Let them come for me.

FIFTY-TWO

I WAKE with a dry mouth and a fuzzy head with the light. I always wake up too early in the van. I peek out. Two people are going to the shower block, but otherwise, there is no life. It's dead at this time of the year.

I check out early, sticking a note with some cash into the site office. I move on to my next site.

I read somewhere that one of the ways investigators find arsonists is by watching who checks out the fire or visits the embers and ruins later. Arsonists love to admire their own work. The investigators know that rubberneckers or anyone taking particular interest in the fire could be a suspect. I don't even look back. I don't head through the town to go past the fire or the wreckage. I go a different way out.

I park up in a layby and sleep again till the afternoon. I wake up to the warmth of the sun on my face through the curtains. I feel calm … until I remember the night before.

I check into the next campsite on the phone, arranging to arrive there outside of reception hours, so I can avoid meeting anyone. They say to park up, give me a bay number, and say they'll see me in the morning for my payment.

I can't get rid of the smoky smell around me. I tie up my hair and find a cap and spray it with perfume. I hope anyone I encounter can't smell me. I put the clothes bag and rucksack in the front passenger seat, hoping the smell won't spread into the sleeping area. Once at the campsite, I head to the laundry to wash the clothes. Again, it's empty, so I use the showers, which are in the same block. The smoky smell comes out with the hot water. It reminds me of the days after I'd been at a nightclub, before the smoking ban.

I need to use the tumble drier, as it's too cold to hang the clothes up, so I'm there late into the night. I only have the radio for company at this site. There is no Wi-Fi here—it's a bit disconcerting. I am keen to know what is happening. My fear of getting caught is building, but I'm tired from all the action of the day and the drink the night before, so I drift off again.

I'm woken by a knock on my door.

How have they found me? I brace for the inevitable.

It is just Jenny, the campsite lady.

'Hi. I'm here to check you in. I didn't wake you, did I?' She looks worried.

I look at my phone. It's eleven in the morning, so I've slept late. 'No, it's fine. I must have fallen back asleep.'

'Three nights, yeah?'

'Yeah, cool.' I pay her for the three nights in full.

I walk to the town, and my phone fires up. I sit and drink a bottle of water on a bench. With a chance of a social media check coming up, I liven up.

'Tragic Fire Kills Local Woman,' reads the local news site. On the radio station's Facebook page, I read, 'Due to the fire, we are operating from home, as the building is damaged. We are unable to air our usual shows until further notice but we will keep in touch via the Facebook page. (Michael).'

Not many people listen to them these days anyway. The Facebook page is where all the news is. I see comments:

'Terrible loss.'

'Tragic, RIP.'

The Social Club Facebook page states they are closed until further notice.

Police are investigating.

Well, they should, of course.

I haven't thought about Kate. I have no feelings for her. No empathy.

People who love her will be sad. Her parents? Did I just feel something?

Tom? No, I'm back to not caring. I am a numb piece of meat.

There will be the post-mortem, of course. Booze? The fall? Or smoke inhalation? Or nothing left to see?

I'm racking them up. I must move on to the last one. I would like to get to the end.

FIFTY-THREE

I've spent a lot of time foraging and researching poisons. I even kept leaves and flowers in jars, and some frozen in containers until I decided what to do. You can't forage for much in November, and most of the things I need are spring and summer poisons. I ruled mushrooms out straightaway. Paddy hates mushrooms; he won't even eat the normal ones.

I considered deadly nightshade and then hemlock. I read that the roots of poison hemlock are sometimes mistaken for wild parsnips, whereas the leaves look like parsley, so it was on my list for a while. Socrates died taking hemlock. It would be a perfect way to kill the common man's philosopher!

I settled on yew, as it's worse when dried, and I knew where I could get it locally year-round.

I HEAD BACK to the site to get the van and take a drive to Fortin-gall. The Fortingall Yew is an ancient yew tree in the churchyard there. It is known for being one of the oldest trees in Britain, or the world, depending on who you talk to. It is about 3,000-years old.

They say locally that Pontius Pilate was born under it and played there when he was a child. I'm standing on ground the man who condemned Jesus stood on—only time separates us.

Clippings from the tree were taken to the Royal Botanical Gardens in Edinburgh to form a mile-long hedge, which, while closer to my home, is too well guarded. Even in Fortingall, you're not allowed to take any of this tree. A fence around it now deters souvenir hunters. Some bits have fallen off on the ground over the fence around it, so I gather up these dried-up pieces. I don't rip anything off the tree (I'm not a savage!). I'm still well-behaved, despite my recent doings.

I can't remember how many leaves I need, so I nip back to the van to check the photocopied pages from the foraging book I got in Hill-head Library. I can't find the photocopied papers in the back of the sparkly notebook. I left them in the flat.

Shit, they are in the kitchen! That bloody phone call from the scammer distracted me.

I need to go back. I debate. I read it before I came out. Is it fifty leaves or fifty grams? I can't remember. I must go get them. But must I, really? It's a bloody five- or six-hour round trip. But they are lying there, like evidence.

I'm pissed off and stressed, driving back in the van. I can't believe I need to go back. I'm mad at myself, but I can't wallop myself while driving. I hit the wheel. I tell myself, 'Don't go too fast.'

I put the radio on full blast, and I'm speeding, but then slowing down to avoid being noticed. I get madder and madder.

So far, I have heard nothing on the radio about the fire. I am tempted to go look.

No, I tell myself. *I don't feel sorry for Kate!* I recall the time she passed my project off as hers.

'That's great work, Angela, and I assume Kate too,' said Bossman. 'Well done, you two,'

'Thanks,' was all she had said.

I shout out the window as I pass through Fife, although no one can hear me for traffic.

'Bloody liar, liar pants on fire!'

Life is too short to wait.

Fourth Section—Perthshire 1

- ~~Kate—dead~~
- ~~Tom—widowed~~
- ~~Chris—dead~~
- ~~Michael—radio station closed~~
- ~~Douglas—Teflon-coated council drunk~~

Club, building, attics

enjoy every moment.

Fifth Section—Perthshire 2

- Paddy
- Linda—monkey
- Denise—monkey
- Mandy—monkey
- Gillian the slut
- Sandra—beauty queen
- Barbara—the next one

Forage, hotel, letter

FIFTY-FOUR

'HAVE YOU BEEN SMOKING?' Preston smelt the smoke off my hair as I brushed past him into his flat. I had washed my clothes well, but not well enough. He'd seen my van in the car park, perhaps heard me banging about upstairs and was waiting on the landing for me when I came down. I was ushered in for a cup of tea.

'It will be from the fire pit; I was eating outdoors,' I reply, thinking fast.

'In November? You are mental.'

'I don't know why I keep forgetting things.' I maintain I came back for something, which is true. He'll think it's the tumour and not pursue that line.

'So, how's the camping? Strangely, I don't love camping.'

'You do ... in a way.' I joke.

'My type of camping is in a five-star hotel with butler service.'

'Did you go to the funeral in the end?'

He nods and smiles.

'How was it?'

I missed Preston's mum's funeral on purpose. I don't mind cemeteries, but I can't cope with the actual ceremony of the death, thank you very much. He guides me to take a seat, and it is clear there is a story to tell.

'I wasn't going to go, but then I decided that if had to go, I wasn't going to fade into the background. My family don't like the gays, which is ironic,' he begins.

'Because of you,' I fill in.

'Aye, and Uncle Geoff and Auntie Jerry, his so-called flatmate for twenty years. But at least they keep up that fakery well enough, so they tolerate them.'

'Ah, and Red too.'

'Red's not gay.' He bites.

I feel stupid for my assumption.

'He hates homosexuals.'

I want more of an explanation. I want to say, 'He raped you.' I open my mouth to speak.

'No.' He nips my question in the bud, and I feel stupid.

'*All* my Family hate them, and *he* hates them the most.'

I pause while I digest this information. 'What happened?'

'I dressed up. I put on my high-heeled boots and a cape. I went as the black widow, like the lassie off the *Scottish Widow*'s advert. I gelled my hair back. I put on full makeup, red lips and dark glasses. I waited till they were all in, and I strutted down the aisle of that church like the drama-queen I am. Here comes the funeral bride! You should have seen their faces. When I got home, I laughed so hard my jaw nearly dislocated like an anaconda.' He is proud, and I clap with delight.

'Anna Conda—is that your drag name?'

'No, that's already taken. It's Bunty.'

'How? I mean, of course. This is a thing.' This is news to me.

'Bunty Van Boudoir.'

'Of course it is. And her signature style?'

'Black widow, as per Mummy's funeral. Or hot pants and roller skates, depending on the occasion. She's an absolute whizz with the sewing machine,' he explains.

'Oh yeah, like that time you took up my curtains?'

'That was Bunty. I love a drape. I wore them for a bit.'

'What, like *The Sound of Music*?'

'No, more like *Gone with the Wind*.'

'I've got to go head back up north. I'm just back to get the fire-lighters and some other stuff.' I don't mention the foraging photocopies.

'Not that bloody journal you're always writing in—or that other one.'

I ignore that. He's not meant to know about them. I'm not talking about that. 'What are you doing today anyway?'

'Going to the vet again,' he replies, looking around for the dog.

'Yeah?'

'My Boaby's not right. He's not himself.'

I still laugh at this. 'Again? You are never away from the vet. When I started blacking out, you told me to take a couple of paraceta-mols and I'd be as right as rain. Two days later, I was in the Western General attached to a drip, getting wheeled in for an MRI. This was you, "Have a wee tablet and a lie down—you're dehydrated with the drink. Just a wee hangover." But the dog or cat sneeze and there's an ambulance at the door.'

'Be still, my beating soul,' we say together. We laugh, and I go and grab what I need.

FIFTY-FIVE

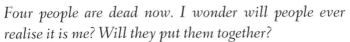

"Four people are dead now. I wonder will people ever realise it is me? Will they put them together?

I was at the nursing home the day before Miss Moleman died, and in Glasgow and on the island at the time of the next two deaths. Mark, of course, might have initiated a murder enquiry if I went too far with the beating, but it could look like an accident. You can't accidentally fall downstairs and not try to save yourself sober. No, he must have taken alcohol at the wedding reception.

It is a shame for Mark's wife and family ... maybe. Sometimes you don't know what goes on behind closed doors. They might feel relieved to be rid of that narcissist in the long run.

Or maybe I'm the narcissist. I'm self-centred and selfish at times. I can inflate an achievement, duck responsibility, or treat people badly now and then, like anyone. I think a true narcissist has a great deal of self-

importance, and I never think I'm good enough, so I can't be.

Am I a psychopath?

Maybe I am a sadist?

Or I could simply violently hate some people who deserve it? I am not fearless like psychopaths are, but I have nothing to lose.

I can still muster some empathy, but not so much that I stop. So, I'm not a psychopath ... but the murders say otherwise.

Maybe I'm a sociopath? Certainly, killing people is antisocial, but I feel rotten after it. I'm not sure it's a guilty conscience.

My head hurts, and then I hurt myself for doing it. I don't know what I am.

AFTER BUYING a mince pie from the bakers, I head north again, back to the campsite. As I drive, I remember how Paddy convinced me I was mad, although he didn't think mental illness was real. He was so convincing that the police believed it, and then the doctors got involved.

Linda was able to report me to the police with complete conviction. With total honesty, I told the doctor that I was insane. I told her my boyfriend said I was crazy. His friends thought so too.

I had no awareness of what I was doing, but I was told I was terrible. I persuaded the doctor I needed a psychiatric referral. Her initial diagnosis was bipolar disorder. I managed to keep down a job, run a home, mother a child, and sing in a band—I must have had a double life.

The psychiatrist saw right through it. By the end of the session, he was asking me about my boyfriend more than myself. I went through all the episodes and explained that my behaviour was terrible, but I was so deluded I couldn't see it. The psychiatrist listened and then stopped the session.

'You can't see it because it isn't happening. You are not bipolar. You are stressed because you have a controlling, possibly narcissist boyfriend.'

'No, you don't understand. Everyone says I'm crazy.'

'You aren't. You've just sat there and complained about a rotten fella. You are bound to be upset.' He smiled. It was good news he was telling me, but I was almost disappointed I couldn't get a pill to take it all away, to fix me so Paddy wouldn't rage at me anymore.

'But there must be something wrong with me, to explain this.'

'If anything, you are suffering from anxiety. You are neurotic, perhaps, but not psychotic.'

'Why did this happen to me? I knew a guy Eric before who was similar, and Steve before that was horrid too. It keeps happening. It must be me!' I didn't get as far back as Mark.

'Well, you picked them.'

It helped me, but it shocked me too. It's not me, but I was still to blame for choosing them. I couldn't see through them.

After I walked out of there, I was amazed at my stupidity for not realising this. I'd wasted this doctor's time. No wonder Paddy didn't want me going to find out I wasn't as crazy as he said.

When I told him, he went back on the 'Mental illness is fake' trip. 'Psychiatrists are keeping themselves in good jobs.' Paddy brushed it off. 'Probably a quack anyway.' He carried on as normal.

'Gaslighting' is the name for it now. He made me believe I was unable to see my own reality clearly. And he'd happily deny any abusive things he said. He'd insist, 'I never said that!' That was that— end of conversation—even if he had admitted saying it hours before. His sudden abuse-amnesia made me further doubt myself.

He was like Eric in that, telling each person a version of the truth, whatever they thought that person wanted or needed to hear. A narcissist, a pathological one.

He always needed a woman to complain about to his monkeys

about, to get the sympathy he craved because, as the narcissist, he was always the victim, always at the centre.

He wasn't an atheist *because* he was a narcissist, but believing in God wasn't compatible with his abuse. If he had been the traveller saved by the Samaritan in the Bible story, he would have abused the Samaritan afterwards. His atheism stemmed from the prolonged process of his religious mother dying when he was a young child; he hated God after that. I managed to get that out of him once, and it made me understand him some. But he didn't want me to analyse him or to explore how his past affected him. He thought he was perfect. 'I'm the best and bonniest boy,' he would say. 'Mother said so.'

I finally reach the campsite at Perthshire late for night two. Perthshire covers a large area, and this campsite is between where I worked and where Paddy lives, about fifteen miles from here. I bed down for the night, exhausted by the journey and the stress of the morning visit to the Fortingall Yew.

IN THE MORNING, I head to the town on the way to Paddy's house and sit in the hotel bar for a while. I close my eyes, recalling a night here where I was 'having too much fun'. That is something else he couldn't stand—whenever I was free, laughing, and being happy. He needed me to care about him and him only.

We stayed here, in Denise's hotel, for the night. It wasn't far from where we lived, but we decided to make a weekend of it, so it would feel like a holiday.

The lads in the band knew me, and after they had finished playing, we got locked in for extra hours of drinking. Paddy never said anything to me in the bar, and he seemed to be enjoying himself. At the time, I wished it could always be like this. I was in a drunk, happy state. I forgot to worry what might happen next, but Paddy always loved the element of surprise. Back in the room, his expression changed.

'You know everyone was laughing at you.'

'What? Who?'

'Those guys were laughing at you. They were only in your company because you were paying for drinks,' he went on as I got changed for bed.

'I can afford it,' I shouted from the ensuite, where I was brushing my teeth.

'They don't care about you,' he shouted back.

'So what? I had fun. It doesn't matter.' I came out, relaxed, and sat on the bed he was lying on. Once I lay down, Paddy sat up. Clearly, he was building up to the usual barrage.

'I saw you had fun, all right. The way you act is embarrassing. Do you not care what people think about you? How that reflects on me?' He stood up.

'How I act?'

'Being loud, laughing so loud! Being drunk, unfeminine, a rowdy!'

'What do you care about how I act?' I whined.

'I'm here, aren't I? Don't I count for anything?'

'Look, I enjoyed myself. I don't know what you think I've done.'

'Done? I could list what you've done. For a start, the way you abused my friends.'

'Oh no, not this. Abused?'

'Yes, abused! A couple of them were here tonight, some you blocked on Facebook, like you did with Denise and Mandy and ...'

'I know what I did. Do you remember why?' I dared interrupt.

'I don't know *why* you do anything. The way you treated Gillian, you were lucky the police didn't take that further and lawyers didn't get involved.'

I thought of mentioning that he had apologised for that episode, and that I'd done nothing illegal. I learnt, during the years I spent in a relationship with Paddy, that I was required to shut up, be nice, and never bring up his behaviour, but I couldn't help it, given the ill-judgment of alcohol.

'The woman you slept with behind her husband's back and my back?'

'I did not.'

'You admitted it, Paddy. You stood in my kitchen and admitted it.' I rolled my eyes.

'No, I never did. You made that whole thing up. You can't even stand me having female friends. You are so jealous and paranoid.'

I was getting the line he fed to the flying monkeys, even though he had told me the truth. I slumped down beside the bed. Paddy leant over me. He was winning.

'The way you went on about Sandra when I hadn't spoken to her for years. The way you spoke about Monica and the kids. The violent behaviour!'

'Violent?'

'Yes, violent.'

'I haven't done anything violent.' The only time I was violent was against myself.

'You would have if I hadn't stopped you.'

'I thought we were starting again—we are moving on now.'

'You need to learn, and I'll not be stopped from telling you.'

'What do you want me to do?'

'You need to show some remorse for your actions.' He folded his arms.

'How?'

'Just learn. Show some humility, some remorse!'

'How? How do I fix this?' I became louder and louder with each question. I climbed out onto the window ledge three flights up. 'I'm sorry. I'm sorry. Is that enough? Do you want me to jump? Is that enough remorse?'

'You are pathetic.' He shook his head. 'Childish drama.' His face hardened, 'Go on, jump.'

I sat on the window ledge, thinking I could stop this. I was so intoxicated I doubted I'd feel a lot. I sat there in the quiet, cold air till he fell asleep. My legs were numb in the night air because all I was wearing was my nightdress.

When I finally climbed back in, I slept on the floor. I was too scared to wake him.

I OPEN MY EYES AGAIN, and I'm fast-forwarded to now. The place looks and smells the same. I feel that if I turn a corner, they will all still be laughing and joking in the bar, with Paddy waiting for me in our room.

After a session like that, I'd be tricked into feeling sorry for him, mainly for ruining his night with my drama-queen activity. That episode became 'the time you got drunk and threatened to jump out a window for attention'. The pity party for him would carry on, and there would never be an apology on his part. If I started to point out his share of the argument, he either said it never happened, or the problem was me not being able to forgive enough. I needed to work on my forgiveness. I needed to be more like that Jesus fellow I liked so much.

'If you love me, then you will let that go,' he'd say with a laugh.

He never let anything go. He stored it up to remember later for more button-pressing. Any apologising would have meant he had to take responsibility, to evolve, to learn from it. In his mind, he had no need to. What he learnt from our relationship was how to hurt me.

I head to the toilet on my way out and leave a tap on with the plug in one of the sinks. I exit via the back stairs.

I know the hotel well, as I'd loaded my band equipment in here once. I set off the fire alarm and then visit the electrical box and flip the fuse switches. That will keep wheezy Denise inconvenienced at least till the end of the day. *Manage that, monkey.*

I post the letter I have, explaining to Linda's husband that she had told me she didn't love him anymore. I signed it 'a friend'.

Mandy married again and looked miserable with it, so she required no follow up.

Gillian's husband had had a stroke; she now was the carer for the man she cheated on.

A quick call to the taxman about Sandra two weeks ago sorted her out. The only time Paddy spoke well of her was talking about the drawers of cash she hid in her house from her side job.

I never knew what became of Barbara, but being wrapped up with Paddy and jeopardising her marriage was enough punishment.

FIFTY-SIX

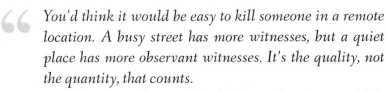

You'd think it would be easy to kill someone in a remote location. A busy street has more witnesses, but a quiet place has more observant witnesses. It's the quality, not the quantity, that counts.

I knew Paddy wouldn't be there when I arrived. He was never one for working a lot, but he had a proper job stacking shelves at a supermarket one day a week. He wouldn't have changed that. He was a creature of habit.

He called himself a self-employed man and had a few ventures here and there. He'd make models and sell them online. He'd try a bit of anything. Or he would take up a job and last a fortnight. He could never take anyone telling him what to do.

Sometimes he'd take on seasonal work in the summer when the tourists came. Sometimes he'd work in the hotel with Denise. I paid for everything with the promise of repayment. I never got any of it back.

Now and again, he'd say when I asked, 'After what

you've put me through, it's the least you can do. In fact, I deserve damages.'

IT IS easy to break into the house. Paddy always left the garage door open in case he forgot his key. His house is remote, situated along a single-track road lined with neighbours, but they are acres apart. After his house, there is a public car park. People park there and have picnics, then stroll through the woods away from his house, along a river, and after four miles come out at a grand house.

If I'm seen, I could pretend I was visiting the local site. It isn't that popular in winter, and although they might not remember individual cars, some nosy neighbours might still notice. I wear a blonde wig—at least that might put them off—but the van is obvious. Another camper van and a couple of cars are there too. I park up. I can walk back to his house from here.

Once I climb over all the junk in Paddy's garage, there is a door to the right, which is, yes, open, and leads into the house. I look back at the garage and remember he told me his daughter slept in here one night after he had thrown her out by the scruff of the neck because she refused to clean her room. He locked out her out of the house in the rain, and he went to bed.

His children were trained like dogs, and he tried to train me like one too. Monica and her man had moved away with the children, now teenagers, not long ago. Paddy had perpetuated the myth his wife had left him and the kids, when, in fact, they shared joint custody. They had stayed with him for two weeks after she left, while she moved house, but that was the best sob story, so he kept that one going for years.

The kids were never there when I visited. The boy was his favourite because the daughter looked like Monica. He said his son was a star. He thought himself a superstar, and his son—his double— could grow to his stature. God forbid if that boy ever let him down.

The house has not changed, even after all those years. How many years since I was here? Six or seven? His house was always a mess. To get me to come back that last time, he promised we would live together in this house and be a proper couple. For some reason, I took him at his word. He said he needed to get the house sorted first, so I set about it. I would help him clean and sort the place—perhaps we'd decorate it, get it looking good.

I cleaned a lot while he sighed. He did not want to throw anything out. I left him in the living room while I set about the filthy bathroom. Under the sink, I found a makeup bag. The daughter's? She was only eleven at the time. There were tampons in there. They weren't his daughter's. She'd have been six when they went out of date five years ago. I put them back.

If Paddy ever felt shame, it was this once. I took a photo of the mess, more to show the benefits of the cleaning—a before-and-after picture. He was enraged. I'd evoked a sense of inadequacy in him. He went on another epic rant and rave, and I recognised he was defending himself excessively. I was cleaning his house, and he was angry with me. I never did move in.

Fresh layers of dust have landed now. Monica's tampons are still there. She must be menopausal by now. I am perimenopausal, and she was a lot older than me.

I look around and see his laptop on the chair. *Good God, it's the same one!* He got to the stage where he didn't even try hiding his women juggling. We'd be watching TV and he would sit with his laptop on his lap and show me all the tabs open to the women he was simultaneously chatting with.

'Why are you doing that?' I'd say as I peered around to check the screen.

'I'm talking to friends.' None of those women knew he was spinning all these chats like plates. I saw he told the exact funny story to all and waited for the reaction. He could have saved a lot of time by cutting and pasting.

I head upstairs to the bedroom, which is unchanged and still untidy. I catch myself in the dusty mirror. I reflect that he'd always demean me instead of criticise constructively. I tried to improve myself, so I was as perfect as he wanted me to be, as perfect as he thought he was. I didn't mirror him, so I needed improvement. That's the thing with a narcissist, they are in love with their own reflection. Any deviation from perfection needs fixing.

I think Paddy knew he didn't measure up to his own image of himself, so most things he threw at me as insults were, in fact, self-assessments.

'You are going to end up very lonely,' he'd say.

I see no sign of any women, but there are condoms in the drawer. Then I spot a dress in the wardrobe—a green dress, which must belong to the current woman. Is this Barbara's? I start laughing when I realise it is mine. My green dress that I wore at the hotel. *Why did he keep this?* I thought I lost it in the move. I take it and stuff it in my bag.

Earlier, I had taken the East Lothian branded wrapper off the shop-bought pie and placed all the dried-up yew inside it, mixed in with the meat. I leave it in the porch, now in a plain bag on which I've written, 'From an admirer—Heat up at 180 degrees for 20 minutes'. He'll put it in the microwave for sure.

I check the fridge, but there is nothing in it apart from some ham. I throw that out, so he'll eat the pie tonight or tomorrow. It's his day off tomorrow. No one will miss him. Anyone who messages won't question Paddy not answering, not with the routine silent treatment he uses.

I RETURN THE FOLLOWING DAY. The green dress doesn't fit any longer, but I put on a coat over the top to cover the back not fastening up. If he is still about, I'll take the frying pan and knock him out.

Clang, clang, clang.

Clang, clang, clang.

I'll do it over and over, like the times I punched myself. As I walk to his house, I punch mid-air in furious anger. I imagine using the frying pan, and I act it out while walking along the path. I check to see if anyone saw. No, the car park is empty. No tourists today.

I find him dead in the living room, on the sofa, clutching his heart. The laptop is still on his knees. I locate the remains of the pie and the note and throw them in the septic tank outside in the garden. The lid is still off. He never did fix it.

I kept telling him the kids or the dog might fall in. His cat disappeared and was never seen again. But no, it is not yet fixed—typical.

I change my plan slightly. I considered this the last, so I could leave him where he died and I could get caught. But why should I?

I drag him to the septic tank. With it being wide open, it's quite easy to get him in there. He sinks into the tank like the piece of shit he is.

Life is too short to wait.

Fifth Section—Perthshire 2

- ~~Paddy—foxglove, mushrooms, hemlock, Socrates, yew~~
- ~~Linda—monkey, letter~~
- ~~Denise—monkey, hotel~~
- ~~Mandy—monkey, married~~
- ~~Gillian the slut—stroke~~
- ~~Sandra—beauty queen, tax~~
- ~~Barbara—the next one~~

Forage, letter, hotel

enjoy every moment.

FIFTY-SEVEN

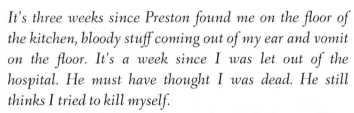

> It's three weeks since Preston found me on the floor of the kitchen, bloody stuff coming out of my ear and vomit on the floor. It's a week since I was let out of the hospital. He must have thought I was dead. He still thinks I tried to kill myself.
>
> Thank God Callum was at his dad's house. He is still there now.
>
> What a year! I put up my Christmas gratitude tree again this week. Have I wasted my time? Aren't we all killing time, all the time? We hate being bored, but that is when we have the most time of all.
>
> I have a lot of time on my hands daily, and I don't like it.
>
> I've tried mindfulness and mindlessness and meditation. They're no use, because I'm a fidget. I fill my time with things that make the time go quicker.
>
> They say life is too short. I look for distractions, like movies and sightseeing, to make it go that little bit quicker, so I can get to the end without ever being bored.

Ever been bored on a boring bus journey? Kill some time
reading. Ever been bored on a long-haul flight? Kill time
by watching a movie. Look at a headstone. Kill some
time.

We concentrate on the start date and the stop date,
but the line in between is when we lived. It may as well
be a dot. The word 'time' should always be preceded by
the word 'precious'. There's more Facebook philosophy
for Brian. Amazing, isn't it? I still talk to him, but at
least now he doesn't answer back.

MY JOURNALING IS STOPPED by Preston coming in.

'Hiya. Just checking you are okay?' he says timidly and softly.

'I'm fine.' I smile.

'Are you, though?' he asks with his gentle counsellor's voice.

'Lots of medication and all sorted,' I say matter-of-factly.

'Okay,' he sighs and speaks more normally. 'I'll keep checking on you, though, and if I text, you must answer. If you don't, I'll just keep coming in.'

He does that anyway.

'With you, John, Susan, Jen, and Callum, I will need to text all day long. I'm honestly fine. I've been writing some things to keep me occupied. How have you been?'

'All right,' he shrugs. 'Nothing much is happening. Red is coming round with some stuff he cleared out of Mum's. He wanted us to sort it together, but I told him to take what he wanted and dump the rest. I asked him for a photo that hung on Mum's living room wall. I always looked at it while I played the piano, and I felt safe. It was as if I was in another place when I played.' He looks into the distance as he remembers. He sighs again, and then he is back in the room with me. 'Wouldn't want any of the rest of the shite.' He brightens up. 'Anyway, enough about me!' As he stands up to leave, he says softly,

'If you need anything, let me know.' He walks to the front door and sees the holdall there.

'I'm going to Tara's this weekend, till Sunday night. I'll be fine there,' I explain.

'Okay. Message me her number. At least you won't be alone. You'll need supervision.'

He thinks I tried to kill myself. I could have, and almost did, but that's not what happened.

My state of unconsciousness, burst eardrum, subsequent vomiting and passing out was a result of my self-harm gone as far as it could go.

FIFTY-EIGHT

 I never should have named him. He developed a personality, and then a voice.

Brian's voice started off positively. To begin with, the things he said were encouraging, kind even. Then his voice changed. He became a hateful bully.

My brain was in shock from the cancer, the previous mental illness, the alcohol, the stress and the drugs I take for anxiety. Suddenly, all I could think of was killing and murder. These weren't vague or passing ideas or random thoughts. I saw them in clear, 3D vision, as if I were sitting at the cinema chained to the seat, forced to watch my horrific actions take place. It was terrifying.

I began the usual way of battering myself. I gave myself the old one-two. One was to distract myself with an endorphin rush, and two was to punish myself for being the monster I am. Three was to deal with them for the last time by punching until I heard something give, a crack in my head to the point of concussion.

When I woke up in the hospital, the questions

started. *I was too tired to lie. My throat was dry and burning from the vomit. I told them everything, and I was transferred to the psychiatric hospital. The doctor noted the voices in my head, but he concentrated on the murders.*

In the psychiatric department, I was placed on my first antipsychotic. It was a special day: I'd finally been promoted to clinically insane.

Brian had grown again, turned nasty and convinced me I was the worst person in the world. Murderers are the worst people in the world, so that's what I became. I remembered all the people who hurt me. Brian told me I was evil enough to kill them all.

Psychoses took over. All I could think of was planning the murders in graphic detail. The doctors told me psychoses are rare in brain cancer. Homicidal ideation is only seen in about 10 per cent of psychotic episodes. I felt quite special.

They are all dead now. To clear things up, I didn't kill them. Brian told me I did, and I filled in all the blanks, trying to remember how, because I knew he was telling the truth. Brian knew how terrible I was, knew I could carry it out with no trouble. The video of how it happened played in my brain, and I believed every second.

I was there—at the nursing home, in Glasgow, on the island, in Perthshire. I did go walking behind the home and visit the old lady the day before she passed away in her sleep. I was in Glasgow when Mark died. I was around when Eric committed suicide and when Kate died in the fire. I went to all these places.

All the events I have written in this journal are real, apart from the murders, which were simply my visions. I was writing to kill time, but that's the only killing I did.

I DON'T HAVE enough time left now to write my memoirs or to finish the bucket list. I started writing in my journal, but all I could think about was the negative things, the terrible emotions. I should have written some more positive things and put them on that bloody gratitude tree. But I have been on a cruise ship, travelled a good part of the world, rescued cats, owned a dog, fronted a band, got a degree, seen an Old Firm game, and taken some classes.

I'm grateful for all I have experienced, sad that I won't experience more, and angry that I will forget all of this before I perish.

I am annoyed that I missed a year believing hallucinations and regurgitating the past, but I'm not getting mad about that now. I saw what use *that* was to me.

I have an idea to use what I wrote in my sparkly notebook and journal, to turn it into a novel, killings and all. That way, I can still be the heroine of a book, in a way.

And I'll have to think of a beginning and an end. I toy with the lead character dying, getting killed, getting caught, or getting away with it and living happily ever after. Then I thought I could invent a pair of detectives on the case, looking for clues. The heroine could leave a calling card at each scene, linking the murders, and they could spend time matching up what they had in common. But I don't know anything about detectives or police and how they work, and it would bother me if procedures weren't right.

They say, 'Write what you know!' The events are real; even those that aren't *seemed* real. I've typed it all out from the sparkly notebook and my journal into Word. I'll need to change names and places and other details. I don't want people recognising themselves or their loved ones.

Of course, no one missed Miss Moleman. Mark was different. Elizabeth and the kids were devastated when he dropped dead of a heart attack at his daughter's wedding and fell down the staircase in the venue where he met me. The cigarettes proved too much for him in the end. I was in Glasgow that day. I thought of going in, but I went to Tina's book launch instead.

Eric did take his own life. I was on the island at the time. I walked around that area, drank a few whiskeys in the pub, and didn't even know he'd driven off till the next day.

Kate's death was, of course, tragic; she was still fairly young. Sadly, her husband didn't notice she hadn't returned, as she would often drink and pass out at work. She had a drinking problem, like her uncle. Tom is already living with his secretary.

Paddy is not officially dead, only missing. I hope they don't find him in the septic tank, or I might start thinking I did it again.

I GET ready to head to Tara's house. I print out two copies of the 'sparkly notebook and journal notes' covering up until I went into hospital. One is for Tara, which I will leave with her to edit and make suggestions. I get my holdall out of the cupboard and put that printed copy in there for her. It's called *The Bucket List* for now. That was why I started it after all—as a bucket list of things to do and Paul's idea of an enemy list. I'll need a better title, but for now, that's it.

I also pack the stolen self-help book. (Yes, I stole that from Tina for real. She owed me money, the thief!) Tara likes that sort of personal improvement stuff, but I've no time left for that now.

I leave the extra copy of the journal notes on my kitchen table to revise on my return. I could work on the Mac, but I prefer a hard copy and a red pen. I'll fix typing mistakes, bad grammar, and any boring, rambling chunks. I don't even recognise what I wrote at times.

Thank God Tara is non-judgmental. She took it in her stride when I told her my cancer made me have psychotic, murderous visions. It seems crazy when I put it in one sentence.

In the end, we don't spend time 'writing novel things' at Tara's. We walk and talk about food, health, men, makeup, and fashion. She says she'll read my words when I go home and call me later with her thoughts. She'll need to get on with it. I might not have too long left. Who knows, though? I might see another year.

I enjoy some quiet time with Tara, but I'm happy to come home in the end. I dump my bag in the kitchen and notice that the other copy of my potential novel is gone. Did I give her two by mistake? Did I accidentally bin it?

It's on Word anyway now, so I print it out again. There are pages and pages of it. I must remember to buy ink and paper. My brain is foggy with cancer sometimes. I worry that the madness is back, and I am forgetting things. Or is it age? Drink? No! I cut that out.

Is it Brian? Or my medication?

As the screeds are printing, I pop out my door, thinking I better check in with Preston. He sent me a message telling me I was to let him know when I was back. On the landing, I can still hear the printer whirring and clunking away in the flat. At that second, Preston messages to say he saw me coming in and to come down.

His door is open. I enter and go straight into the kitchen, which is directly below mine.

I get no, 'Hiya,' no flamboyance. I notice he smells of lime and lemon. He is fresh out of the shower, his hair still wet. I don't see Willie, but Boaby barks from one of the bedrooms, where he appears to be locked in, for some reason.

'I read your journal. The printed one,' Preston says, ashen.

'You took it?' I roll my eyes. *I knew I left it on the kitchen table!* I'm relieved I'm not going mad (again).

'Yeah, I read it. Most of it.'

I plonk myself down at the table. 'Fuck's sake, Preston, I was looking for that. I thought I was losing my marbles.'

'Too late, love,' he jokes. Then he adds more seriously, 'I needed to know you were okay.'

'Okay, so you stole it, Johnny Light-fingers ... and made me wonder if I was going mad all over again,' I reply in mild indignation, although I'm glad there is an explanation and I didn't imagine the whole thing.

'You were so secretive about what you were writing in that sparkly book. I saw you stuff it in drawers and cover it up with papers. Then you were traipsing about all those places on your own. I came up on Friday, later on, to make sure you'd gone to Tara's and hadn't stuck your head in the oven.'

'It's electric,' I interject, but he doesn't stop.

'I saw "Sparkly Notebook and Journal Notes" on it, and I thought I'd see what you were up to ... Why you tried to kill yourself.'

'I didn't try to kill myself,' I manage to butt in.

'That was why you were in hospital.'

'No. I got ill with the tumour, and it made me mental. And then I was writing all about my life for my memoirs. It was on the bucket list of stuff to do before I was fifty or dead, but all the shit things came out. And I ...' I sigh. I was about to say, 'Knocked myself out,' when he interrupted.

'I know. I read it.' He pauses, and my head drops.

'Oh God, do you think I'm awful?'

'No, they deserved it.'

I manage to laugh. 'Ha-ha, they did. They all did.' He looks at me in admiration. 'Still, it's not good for me to go over all that. I wasn't right in the head. Brian had a voice, and it all came out.'

'Aye, that was a bit weird ... the Brian bit.' He stares at the top of my head, as if he might see him. 'What does he sound like? Is he Scottish?'

'I don't know.'

'I think he sounds like Sean Connery, no' sure why. Never mind. You're okay now. And those bastards are all dead. They can't hurt you now.'

'What? ... Yeah, they are all dead.'

'Right.' He lets out a huge sigh and shakes his head. 'My God, though ...'

'I don't want to keep talking about it,' I say.

'Okay. How was Tara?' He changes the subject.

'Usual.' I try to change the subject again, away from me. 'Has

Red been? Your brother was coming with a picture or something on Saturday.'

'Yes. He brought some photo albums and things. I asked for one bloody photo off the wall, and I got a whole suitcase-worth from the attic. Couldn't even follow a simple instruction. Then he said I could bring the ones I didn't want back next week. I thought I am never going to be free of this bloody human. I wished I'd never asked for anything,' he says huffily.

'Are you going to cut him off now? I think enough is enough,' I say. But Preston carries on, 'Red just stood there as I flipped through the photos, and it brought it all back. He was leaning over my shoulder, breathing on me, looking at the photos of when we were young ... all as if nothing happened.' He is talking at a hundred miles an hour now, and he has been standing or pacing the whole time.

'Oh, Preston, are you okay?'

'I am fine. I think. I'm surprised at how fine I am—but God, he was in my flat with me on my own ... Anyway, the photos.' A box sits on the kitchen table I am sitting at.

'I have them here,' he says. 'I need to speak to you about something.' He takes a deep breath. 'The Man.'

'What man?'

'Your man! *The* Man. I found him, Angela.'

I try to decipher what he is referring to.

'What do you mean, "You found The Man?"'

'Okay. It's in here, in your journal.' He holds up my papers. 'When you were a wee kiddie.'

'Oh God, that guy. Oh ... well.' *Oh hell no, I'm not talking about this.* 'Shit happens to a lot of people. You should know that.'

'I know who he is.'

'Don't be daft. He was a man in the 1970s in North Berwick. Could be anyone.'

'What campsite was it?'

'The top one. Up the hill.'

'We had a caravan there,' he says.

'Who did?'

'Mum and Dad.'

'So what? You wouldn't have been there when I was there.'

'But Mum and Dad were. They had the caravan for ages after I left home. We would go there every year, and they kept going. They could have been there with him, my brother, or he could have gone on his own. He had a key. That's where they put him when they moved him out. He matches the description in here.'

'God. That's too much of a stretch. You don't think it's him?'

'He is tall.'

'Everyone is tall when you are eight!' I am up and pacing now.

'Ginger.' He hands me a picture.

I can't see The Man's features in my mind, but I try to remember. His face is a blur to me. Then I look down at the photo, and it all comes into focus. I see him here in my hand. I'm looking right at him.

'I don't know.' I want to run away. Is this an adrenaline fight or flight moment? With all these meds? How can this feeling be penetrating through the drugs? *God, I feel sick.*

The underwater feeling is back and is blurring my vision and hearing. I know from what Preston says and the photo that Red is guilty, but I can't deal with him being The Man. Look what I might have done to the others, who are, thankfully, dead already.

'I don't know. It's a while ago,' I mumble unconvincingly.

'If I had stopped him, stabbed him in the hospital, then he wouldn't have done that to you.'

'It's maybe not him.' I feel my face is red. I've done nothing to indicate this is not him, so Preston knows he is right.

'I should have stopped him years ago.'

'We should go to the police,' I say. 'Your mum is gone, but they can sort these things out now. People get convicted years after the event, and they won't say, "Why did you leave it so long?" I'll say I didn't know where he was, and you can say about your mum dying, the journal jogging your memory, and they'll understand. I'll come with you.' I gain a bit of clarity and try to claw some sense back into the conversation.

'No!' Preston shouts. He jumps up.

I am shocked at the macho, manly voice that yells at me. 'You can't go to the police. No one knows you did all this. No one knows at all, or they'd be here already.' He gestures to the window.

I meant he should let them know about Red. I don't know where what I've done comes into it. I'm frozen to the spot.

Bang, bang, thump, thump. My blood is so noisy. My chest is loud with the thumping. It feels like someone standing on my throat to stop the air. *He thinks I killed those people. He's read it as truth!*

Why wouldn't he? All of the words in it are true. We had all those conversations, and he knows I went to Glasgow and away in the van. He was there for all of it. Preston saw the leaflets from the nursing home, Tina's book, the green dress. He smelt the smoke off my hair.

Preston knows some of these people. He knows that Susan and Paul, Jen and Jill are real.

How can I feel this anxious when I'm cured and on all this medication?

I start to explain that my tumour made me imagine all the killings, but he keeps speaking, as usual, and I can't get a word in. I can't find the words, and I'm slower than normal with these drugs.

'I've fixed everything, but it's not done right. I can't think like you in advance and work out all the possible scenarios and cover things up. I did it all wrong! I should have thought ahead,' he jabbers on and on.

I can't get out the words that I didn't kill anyone. My mouth is so arid. My tongue is stuck to my palate and my teeth to my lips. It's a side-effect of the drugs, but I'm panicking too, and I can't swallow.

I'm tired. I need to be sharp to get a word in at the best of times, and I'm missing this sharpness.

I see his lips moving, but I'm not taking his words in. I've been so slow to understand that he didn't get that all the murdering was fantasy—Brian's fantasy. 'What's happening?' I manage to get out.

'I know about *you*, and I knew you could help *me*,' he says. Preston often talks in riddles, but I'm not getting the joke.

'What do you mean *help you*? How?'

'I need you to help me. I've done it like you ... Oh God, the mess,' he babbles urgently. He is panicking now. He beckons me to follow him along the corridor.

I follow, but I don't know what my legs are doing. I'm walking on soft sponge, and the backs of my knees are tingling. I follow him into the living room.

By the desk, a figure is sitting on the swivel seat facing the window. I can see the back of his head. He's been here the whole time. Preston swings the office chair around, and the figure slumps, his head back, his mouth gaping. Blood smears at the corners of his mouth have dried in an upwards direction, giving him a strange, almost happy look. Another upturned blood smile-gash grins from his neck. In slow motion, my legs go numb, and I am on my knees, staring at it all.

My eyes lower to his collar; blood specks smatter his checked shirt and his dark tank top. No, he isn't wearing a tank top. It's wet—wet with blood, giving him a dark vest that smells of raw meat and rusted metal. I can almost taste it in the back of my throat. I gag.

His arms are dangling straight down and limp, with nicotine-stained hands and fingernails at the end. His legs are apart, and his feet are twisted at an uncomfortable angle. I look back up again. He is a big man in a tan-brown leather jacket almost the colour of the chair, and on top a shock of red hair—the reddest I have ever seen.

Red.

Preston's face appears in front of mine. 'I thought I'd ask you how to get rid of the body.'

Life is
too short
to wait.

Sixth Section

- ~~The Man~~

enjoy
every
moment.

EPILOGUE

'I didn't like the ending.'

Well, endings are difficult—all endings. Death just happens. There is neither a grand finale nor enough build-up, unless you are like me.

That is why everyone is so distraught. We were all in denial the whole time.

When it ends in an unsatisfactory fashion, there is loss. There is the 'Why?'

In real life, there are no nicely tied-up denouements. In real life, it just stops.

And everything else keeps going, unravelling like a serial soap. Houses keep getting cleaned. Pets keep getting fed. Hearts keep getting broken. Lists keep getting checked off.

Yes, I'm dying. Everyone is.

But at least I finally managed to take out the bins.

ABOUT THE AUTHOR

Emelle Adams lives in East Lothian with her son and white cat.

Printed in Great Britain
by Amazon

10321024R00164